Silver
SANTA
SILVER BROTHERS SECURITIES

# LACEY SILKS

MYLIT
PUBLISHING

May all your dirty
Christmas wishes come true

"I don't know how I ended up here tonight, with you, but this moment...right now...is all I can think about. It feels...good, right, overwhelming."
Laura Young, Silver Santa

When Laura lands a job as a security guard at the Silver family's luxurious lodge during Christmas, she knows better than to get involved with one of the guests - or does she? All bets are off when she meets James Silver, a disarmingly handsome single father who sparks a whirlwind romance that promises to be the greatest adventure of Laura's life.

*Silver Santa* is the first novel in the *Silver Brothers Securities Family Saga* and a prequel to *Silver Fox.*

# Chapter 1



$\mathcal{A}$ high-pitched squeal pierced through the lobby, grabbing my attention. I twisted on my heel, nearly slipping as a little girl darted out of the lodge, bounding over the threshold like a fearless mountaineer. My eyes remained locked on her, marveling at her tiny legs as they darted across the snow-covered terrain until she hit a patch of ice and lost her balance. I sprang forward, swooping her up into my arms before she hit the ground. "Whoa there, little one! You almost took a tumble." I held her tightly in my arms, right over my hip, the way I'd seen mothers do.

Her dark wavy hair blew in the gentle breeze and she looked up. Her brown eyes stretched wide as she took in my outfit. "You're pretty." She smiled. "Are you Santa's helper?"

"No, but I am part of the Christmas team. I'm a nutcracker."

"From Mr. Tchaikovsky's story?"

She pronounced the last name expertly, and I leaned back.

"That's right. How do you know about Tchaikovsky?"

"I'll go get Mrs. Silver." Allie interjected. We were working security detail for the Silver family and guests, but partnering with my best friend never felt like a job.

"I saw the play. The girl in the story becomes friends with the nutcracker to fight the evil Mouse King."

I'd honestly forgotten the story until she brought it up.

"And does she run outside and slip on ice?" I tickled her ribcage.

She giggled.

"No. Did you know fifty-six percent of kids slip on ice and fall?" she asked.

"Those are some big numbers for your size. How old are you?"

She removed her mitten and spread out all of her fingers, stating, "Five."

My heart clenched inward.

"Kensi? Kensi, where are you?" Teresa Silver called from the inside.

I walked indoors with Kensi in my arms.

Allie returned to our post.

"There you are. Kensi, you're gonna get sick before Santa arrives."

Kensi wiggled to get down before addressing her grand-mother, . "I wanted to see the snow. And daddy will be here soon. He promised a snowman."

Mrs. Silver smiled with kind eyes.

"Daddy never breaks promises, but he won't be happy if you catch a cold. Thank you so much for finding her, Ms...."

"Laura Young."

"Aha, that's right. Welcome to the Silver Lodge. Make your-selves at home, ladies. I need to get this little muffin hot tea with lemon and honey before she catches a cold."

She gave Kensi a mock-stern look, and the little girl giggled.

"Thank you for having us."

Teresa Silver headed toward the kitchen with Kensi, and I returned to my post outside.

"Here they come," I whispered to Allie.

Across from me, she beamed in her nutcracker getup.

"Stay still," she scolded. "I hope I'm half as funny-looking as you." Her fancy nutcracker outfit clung to her body perfectly, accentuating her curves.

"You look like...a nut," I said.

She shushed me and gave me the once-over from the bottom-up. She met my gaze with hers, and screwed up her face like a clown.

"Stop making me laugh. We're supposed to be invisible."

"Good luck in that costume."

She was right. We might just as well be wearing neon signs.

Eight sets of headlights cut through the darkness, gleaming off the crisp snow that crackled beneath eight large vehicles. The snow was piled so high this winter that making a fortress above the town below appeared to be no feat at all. White Christmas, with its flurry of snowflakes and cold-nipped noses, would make for a glorious sight. And after New Year, I was starting my dream job alongside my best friend and work wife, so life couldn't get any better.

The bullet-proof SUVs crept around the bend and parked at the curb.

The faint hum of the electric engines echoed through the air.

As the eighth black SUV pulled up to the curb and the first door opened, Allie and I grabbed a door handle each at the lodge's entrance and stepped back. Cheerful holiday music rolled out from within the lobby. Elaborate decorations of red, green and silver, and sparkling lights strung in elegant patterns, cast a warm and inviting glow. The familiar smell of Gucci wafted through the air, bringing back a distant memory of past visits. I had been here as a kid.

My parents had sprung for private classes and the best gear money could buy, so skiing was a breeze. This security job they arranged for me before joining the force was not only a bid to maintain peace, but also a step toward full independence.

When I moved out of their house two years ago, they were

upset; they thought I should have become a doctor like them, instead of choosing such a dangerous line of work. Yet, here I was, at this magnificent resort, surrounded by opulence that far surpassed those of the hotels we stayed in growing up. Although Cindy and Karl Young were well-off, none of the hotels we visited came close to this luxurious resort's level of grandeur. My mother and father might be rich, but there's a stark contrast between a millionaire and billionaire.

"Behave yourself this evening," Allie uttered under her breath.

"When do I ever misbehave?" I asked, forcing a deep breath into my lungs. I squared my shoulders, taking my position. We had two hours of security detail left.

The first bachelor stepped out of a vehicle and held the back door open. His broad shoulders filled out the cotton turtleneck sweater, each bulging bicep visible underneath the fabric. I took in his fitted black jeans and a stunning, tight posterior. Colorado never looked better.

"Psst, Laura!" Allie whispered and my spine snapped to its original position.

My heart hammered in my chest, and I shifted to see his reflection in the glass door Allie held steady.

Another bachelor escorted a woman out of the car, her hand clutching his arm. Dressed in an all white outfit, she gripped his elbow and waited with her chin held high. The furry snow jacket, white leggings, and Wookie boots, though ill-suited, complemented her figure. Her raven hair spilled over the fur in straight wisps. Another woman emerged from the car. This one was a blonde twin of the first, but the exact opposite. Her black jacket, skintight leather pants, and black Wookie boots were a contrast to her sister's. They each held one of his arms as he slowly led them forward into the fresh snow floating around them. It looked like a scene from a movie, and I couldn't stop staring. Again. The remaining Silver men left the vehicles, some with partners, others alone, as the first man who strolled toward the entrance, turned around and bellowed. "Hurry up! We're late as it is."

The sound of his deep voice sent a chill down my spine, and as he walked toward the building. His hard lips, chiseled cheekbones, and neatly trimmed facial hair gave him a James Bond look. I gaped as he lifted the aviator sunglasses to the top of his head. His face was gorgeous, and his light blue eyes seemed like they could see into my soul. Nervous flutters filled my stomach the closer he approached.

Allie must have sensed my unease because she moved the door, cutting off the reflection.

"Get a grip, Laura. And. Be. Quiet," she mouthed.

Right.

We'd signed contracts and agreements not to disclose details about this event and the attendees.

Three wealthy families, each with multiple kids and grandkids, had arrived for the holiday—all now part of Silver Securities, et al. They formed the prestigious company of the best private investigators, bodyguards, and lawyers in the country.

The group strolled from the car to the entrance with grace, elegance, and sophistication befitting them. The twins exuded all the wealth the Silvers had, except it wasn't theirs. Money wasn't everything, though. The Silver brothers had class and style, and just enough arrogance to show it off. The smell of expensive cologne filled the air, wafting around us and sucking me into their aura.

The front man's strong profile was immaculate - a chiseled jawline, gentle gray stubble and a streak of silver in his hair. He didn't look like my type. In fact, he looked like everyone's type. The type you absolutely couldn't resist.

The lodge manager came forward to welcome the group.

"Good evening, Mr. Silver. Your suites are all ready."

"Thanks, George. What's the forecast?"

"New snow last night and bright skies tomorrow."

He scrunched his brow, as if he didn't enjoy hearing about either fresh snow or sunny days. I pondered what that might mean. Perhaps, he was someone I'd want to stay away from, after all. Besides, he had at least a decade and a half on me, and I was on the job. Mr. Silver was everything I didn't need.

"Thanks again, George."

I assumed he would go inside, but he turned his head toward me. My heart stopped for a moment.

"Nutcracker?" He tilted his neck, so I just shrugged.

*Bastard!* As per the contract, I couldn't talk to the Silvers or their guests, and judging by the smirk on his face, he knew it.

He shook his head and turned to the others by the curb, yelling out. "Who made Hunter responsible for decorations?"

And without thinking, I blurted, "They're beautiful inside."

The words came out before I could stop them, and my hand flew to my mouth in regret. He focused on my face, and my heart sank—until I noticed his curving lip. The silver strand of hair hanging to just beyond his brow completed his I'd-fuck-you-if-I-wanted-to look. My knees went weak.

"I'm sorry," I whispered, and sealed my lips in a thin line.

"It's all right." The corner of his mouth lifted. Thankfully, his other, equally gorgeous brothers and cousins approached to distract him.

The guy with the twins abruptly let them go and ran forward, sliding on his shoes to a stop beside us. He was a younger version of the guy I'd just offended, and I could tell he would be the life of this Christmas party. He patted who I assumed was his older brother on his back. "You're welcome to lift the burden off my shoulders next year, James."

*James.* James Silver. Not exactly Bond, but still, an amazing name.

My attention flew back to the twins, tip-toeing across the

snow in their impractical, high-heeled Wookie boots as they made a beeline for Hunter and James. Tittering, they each grabbed one of their arms with a squeal. James sighed, and with reluctance, he and the Silvers walked inside, making a beeline to the welcome table set with eggnog, tea, and other beverages. I let go of the breath I'd been holding. What on earth was going on?

"Twenty more minutes, and we're done." Allie closed the front door.

We waited for the bellhop to finish unloading the luggage before pulling the door open for him again. Over the next hour, they unloaded one cart full of suitcases after another. The cars pulled away, and we walked around the building's perimeter, checking for threats. We were in the middle of the Colorado mountains. The only threats here were mountain lions and bears. And two nutcrackers. My watch beeped, showing the last fifteen minutes of our shift.

"I can't believe your parents know the Silvers." Allie stepped from one foot to the other, trying to warm up.

"And I can't believe they gave us a twelve-hour notice about this gig." My breath left a trail in the air, and I rubbed my mittens together. The temperature had dropped a few degrees since an hour ago.

"Sometimes, I'm so happy your parents are millionaires."

"It's not as luxurious as it sounds. More money means more problems and less time. Also, the wealthiest one percent own half of the world's wealth. My parents are insignificant compared to the Silvers."

"They still got us this job."

"Right." Despite our falling out, my parents had attempted to reconnect, but I wasn't ready to forgive them. Setting me up with this job was their way of reaching out. But the scars they drew over my body and my heart were so deep, I wasn't ready to forgive them. I knew I would never forget. But they were still my parents. And they were trying, so that had to count for something.

Allie glanced through a side lobby window. "Rumor has it Silver Securities disagreed with one of their partners, so it seems like everyone has issues. Even billionaires."

"As long as we're paid, I don't care about any of that."

We walked around the building and back to the front door, checking for footprints. There were none, but the continuous snowfall covered tracks within seconds.

"Skiing should be fun tomorrow." Allie kicked up a patch of snow and formed it into a ball.

"I know. I can't wait."

"What are you doing with the two grand you earn?" she asked.

I'd weighed the pros and cons of my current situation plenty: paying off my credit card or saving up for a new car. It had been a while since I'd treated myself to a new pair of heels, and the idea of having a shiny new toy and shoes lit a spark in my chest.

"I'm not sure. I'll save some and I'll spend some. Maybe I should ask Santa for the car I need. What about you?"

Allie grinned from ear to ear. "I'm more interested in the intel the Silvers can get me. It's time to map out the road to my happiness. Tristan's the one who leads the group, so I'll start at the top."

I sighed and shook my head.

Allie had no intention of finding happiness in a billionaire's bed. She'd raised too many walls for that to happen. She needed the money, but that wasn't what she desired most, either. Allie wanted safety, intel, and revenge. And knowing my best friend, she'd get it all. Come January, I would work alongside this kick-ass woman on the police force.

"I can't wait to take off this costume and soak in a bubble bath".

"You soak and I'll steam. I hear the sauna calling my name." She winced in pain.

"Is your gut still giving you trouble?" I asked.

She'd been running to the bathroom all day.

"I think it's the chicken nuggets from last night."

"Still?"

Her face twisted with pain.

"It's a good thing I stuck to my fancy grilled cheese."

I couldn't resist ordering the Brie dish my nanny used to make. My indulgence saved me from whatever bug Allie was struggling with—her pink cheeks, kissed by the night's chill, quickly turned an ashen color.

"Why don't you take it easy tonight?"

She gave me a look that could kill.

"I can't take it easy. This is the opportunity I've been waiting for. You think it's a coincidence we got this gig?" She straightened, obviously fighting pain. "It's fate. Let's change and mingle. I feel like tequila would help."

I cringed at the mention. Allie and her damn tequila! She didn't consume much alcohol, but when she did, it was a battle. She had a good reason to drown her troubles from time to time. I would drink daily if a stalker were after me and my mother.

"What happened to the 'keep a low profile' plan for tonight?" I parroted her words back in an unconvincing falsetto, which made her laugh. I hung up our coats in the lobby and we headed left, away from the crowd.

"Tequila will surely make me more presentable, don't you think?" She massaged her hand over her stomach. "And we are officially off duty, so may as well enjoy all the perks. Argh!" She grabbed her mid-section and doubled over.

"The only perk you're enjoying tonight is a comfortable bed."

I lifted her under her arm and led her to the stairwell. Hindsight twenty-twenty, we should have taken the elevator, but I didn't want to risk running into anyone in our silly outfits. The wooden steps creaked, and the number of risers appeared to double as we looked back. We'd reached the second floor landing when a deep laugh resonated from the hallway.

"Hold on."

I peered through the door slit.

There he stood, tall and lean, bracing his arm against a wall near the blonde twin. The other one fiddled with her purse, searching for something. His white shirt was tight over his body, accentuating his broad shoulders. He'd changed into tailor-made pants, which curved around his tight ass.

James Silver was leaning against the wall, his back straight and his arm resting at his side. He looked like he belonged there. He looked like he belonged everywhere. He didn't wait for opportunities. He created them. James scrolled through his phone as the blonde took over and fiddled with their key cards. She tried knocking on the door, as if that would help. Her sister finally pushed the door open with a cry of delight.

"C'mon, Cece. Let's get the tub filled." The fair-haired girl grabbed her twin's hand.

"Have fun, ladies. Hunter's on his way up," James called after them.

"No, no," she whined. "You're coming with us, James." She pulled on his arm.

He unclasped her fingers from around his arm. "I'm sorry, but it's been a long trip. I promise, my younger brother will be here soon."

He slowly pulled the door closed in front of her face, and turned toward the elevators.

Allie gaped. "He left the twins? That's impressive."

"I'm not looking to be impressed," I said.

"What are you looking for?" she asked as she pulled the door from the stairwell open.

"I'm just looking to relax and ski," I said louder than intended, and he heard me. He stopped, turned in our direction, and our eyes met. I held his stare until he broke it and disappeared inside the elevator.

"Men like him know what they want," I whispered to no one.

As the elevator door closed, the sound that came out of Allie next shouldn't be wished on one's worst enemy. Yet, here she was, folding in half, emitting a sound like fingernails on a chalkboard, amplified by a thousand.

The high-pitched shriek made me jump. "We should get a doctor."

I helped her stand up.

"No need. I'll be okay. I just need to rest."

"I know your appendix is gone…"

"I already said—it's those nuggets inside me that need to come out. And I think they're coming out right now."

She moaned like she was dying, but made it to the toilet in time. I held her hair as she threw up, then helped her into the shower, followed by her pajamas.

"Let me get you some tea. Stay here, okay?"

"Not yet. Maybe later." Her voice was faint, and her lips pale. I ran my fingers through her hair and checked her burning forehead. A few more breaths passed before she was sound asleep. I grabbed an ice pack from the small fridge in our room, wrapped it in a towel, and set it gently over her forehead. I tucked her in, shed my nutcracker costume and put on a dress, and went to find tea, but when I opened the door, I bumped into a solid chest.

# Chapter 2
### James

Her delicate scent hit me just before she bounced off my chest. She took a step back, her doe eyes looking momentarily lost. I realized I'd been standing too close and should have backed away, but now that we were here, I'd take advantage of every second her body was near mine.

"I'm sorry. I didn't see you there." Her soft voice hummed, and her cheeks turned a delicate shade of pink.

Eavesdropping wasn't in my nature, but the nutcracker was far more interesting than the twins. Hunter hired the escorts, forcing me to babysit women who came to the lodge for one reason—or maybe two—my dick and free skiing.

"No worries. I heard a cry." My eyes darted toward the faint sounds of someone in distress. "Is everything okay in there?"

"Not really. My friend is sick." She looked back over her shoulder. "She's been having stomach issues all day, and it got worse tonight."

"What can I do to help? We can call a doctor."

"She needs to rest, and I'm on my way to get tea."

"I'll call for room service."

I reached for my phone, but she stopped me with a hand on my wrist. The touch of her delicate, icy fingers on my skin alerted my senses, and my body stirred. She nodded in appreciation before quickly removing her hand.

"No need to bother staff members on Christmas. I can get it myself."

Her unyielding eyes told me it was pointless to argue. Instead, I nodded, then touched the small of her back, guiding her down the hall before she changed her mind.

The elevator door opened, but she halted me with a question. "What were you doing near my room again?"

"I heard a painful wail and I was concerned." The semi-lie burned in my throat. I was concerned, but I also wanted to see the nutcracker again.

"That was Allie," she replied, satisfied with my lie.

Truth is, I was going to knock on the nutcracker's door, either way. She'd captivated me the moment I saw her. I couldn't put my finger on it, but it felt like we'd met before.

"Let's get her that tea. I know the perfect blend." I pressed the main floor button. "The last thing we want is her suffering during Christmas."

My face softened, and her shoulders relaxed.

"You don't know what's wrong with her?"

"No, she mentioned nuggets from last night and food poisoning."

My nostrils flared. I unconsciously loosened my collar and cracked my knuckles. Food poisoning at this lodge was unacceptable. The elevator dinged and opened its doors.

"I have the perfect remedy for whatever's ailing her. And if she gets worse, we'll call a doctor." I stepped into the Christmas themed elevator and motioned for her to join me. The sound of festive jingle bells played over the speakers.

*Fucking food poisoning?*

"What's wrong? You don't like Christmas decorations?"

I caught the reflection of my anger in the mirrored wall.

"No, it's not that. I don't like spoiled food at my resort, and I don't like your friend getting sick. Now, let's grab that tea and get you back to enjoying your evening with me."

Her breath hitched again. "That was smooth."

I winked her way. "Thanks, I try."

The elevator dinged, and the doors opened. I walked alongside her to the lounge and ordered a Silver emergency blend before guiding her to the cushioned seats near the fireplace. Laura glanced around, anxious.

"What about your daughter? Won't she be wondering where you are?" Her eyes lit up with curiosity.

I shook my head in response. "Daughter?" I never mentioned Kensi.

"The one in a fluffy jacket and Wookie boots." She gave me an innocent smile, and I let out an amused chuckle.

"I was unaware you do comedy for a living, Ms. Young."

She laughed. "My apologies. That was quite rude of me. Both twins looked like your type."

I laughed harder; Cece and Candy weren't my type at all. My life was my family, health, and work, leaving no room for a partner.

"She could easily be your daughter." She tilted sideways, crossed one leg over the other, and leaned back in her chair. My eyes followed the length of her toned legs. The dress complimented her figure.

I looked her over and lifted an eyebrow. "How old are you?"

"Twenty-three."

I caught her staring at the silver streak in my hair—a genetic trait shared by me and my brothers since birth—that hinted at my true age. The light stubble over my chin didn't help.

"How old are you?" She bit her lip, then hastily added, "I told you mine, so it's only fair—"

"Thirty-four."

Her lips formed a perfect 'O,' which made me imagine us in

a different position. Alone. By the fireplace. Her on her knees with her beautiful mouth wide open, looking up.

Laura looked me over before her gaze flew back to my groin, where I was hard. *How could I not be?* She was everything a man could want.

I watched as she fought to swallow. "That's not old."

"I'm glad you think so, but I still can't imagine you policing the streets. You're young, and experience takes time. Do they even train you for the real world?"

She laughed and waved her hand. "Nah, they just let us go wild." However, when she bit her lip and took a deep breath, I could tell she was pulling my leg.

"I hope you're kidding."

"Don't worry, Mr. Silver; this nutcracker knows what she's doing. And she can protect you from anything lurking beyond that front door."

"You're pointing to the back."

Her head snapped in that direction, and we both laughed out loud.

"Why do you want to be a cop?" I asked.

"It's a rebellious act against my doctor parents. They're not pleased health care wasn't my calling, but they're trying. It hasn't been easy..."

She trailed off. A distant look passed over her face. I wanted to ask more about her parents, but a cheer sounded from the bar, and she snapped out of her daze, pasting a smile on her face.

"So, now that we've established you don't have twin daughters, is there a wife in the picture?"

A hearty chuckle left me as I locked eyes with hers, letting go of the question I wanted to ask her. Instead, I leaned in and heard my chest vibrate. "Let's make something clear. I would never cheat on my wife with any twin or triplet. So no, I'm not involved with anyone."

"One-night stands only?" she asked.

"Are you offering?"

"Would you take it?"

I leaned back.

"A stupid man wouldn't."

She must have liked that. Her big brown eyes widened, reflecting the Christmas lights around us.

"You look cute when you're feisty, but it won't suit you in law enforcement."

"Why is that?"

"Criminals will eat you up."

"I didn't know you did background checks on nutcrackers... I guess that's how you know I'm going into law enforcement."

"We verify all the nuts out there."

"Interesting."

Laughter and conversation floated across the room, where my siblings and cousins mingled at the bar. Hunter sat between two ladies, happily chatting with Scar and Cash, my younger brothers. I looked at my company and grinned from ear to ear. Laura was incomparable to Cece and Candy.

"You have a fan on the other side." Laura pointed to a sitting area near the Christmas tree.

I looked over at the two-way fireplace and spotted Emma, sneaking glances at us while sipping on hot chocolate.

"That's my little cousin, Emma, with my parents, aunt, and uncle."

Laura pulled her shoulders inward.

"I love family Christmas."

"Yet, you're here on a job."

"I'm here because I need the money."

"Fair enough. Hopefully, you'll find time to enjoy the hills."

"That's if my ski partner gets well. I must admit that being in a mountain cabin near a ski hill has its perks. My parents took me here a few times as a kid, but it's been a while since I skied."

"Where did you ski before?"

She flashed a wide smile, but then bit her lip. "Vermont ski trips aren't as thrilling as what I'm expecting tomorrow," she said, "but I can't leave Allie on her own. Perhaps the tea will help."

She fidgeted in her seat.

"Are you uncomfortable?" I asked.

"I feel out of place here. Everyone is so well dressed."

The sequined dresses sparkled, and jewels shone. Axel Wagner was puffing a cigar outside, and its chocolate scent carried as his brother Ace opened the door and joined him.

I leaned in with a whisper, "You look beautiful."

She blushed.

"This is what results from leaving my younger brother in charge," I explained, checking the tea order on my watch. "The reading room lounge is quiet. We'll grab the tea on the way."

"Are you trying to get me alone?"

*Maybe. Likely. Yes.*

I lowered my elbows to my knees and shifted closer. "How about I tell you exactly what I want, and you tell me exactly what you want? We can skip everything else in between."

She raised her eyebrow. "What's in between the lines here? I want to make sure I'm making a wise choice."

I had definitely made a wise choice to spend my evening with Laura Young. My new year brought on an overwhelming future in Silver Securities, and I wanted a restful vacation… So, why not?

"The in between stuff includes me telling you I'm single, and I'd love to get to know you this Christmas. No strings attached—unless I'm too old for you."

Her cheeks flushed with heat. "So… I would be a distraction from your wife?" she joked.

I fought the urge to roll my eyes. Something about her comments seemed childish, yet strangely charming, all at once. She was a tease, and she didn't know it. But I was patient.

I took her hand and lifted her palm to my lips, saying, "Let's start over." I kissed the top of her hand.

"Fox Silver. My friends call me James, but you already know that."

A small sense of trust filled her eyes. "Laura Young," she said as she dragged her hand back. "I'm here with my friend. She's sick. But you already know that." Laura gestured somewhere upstairs before adding, "Sorry about the wife and girlfriend jokes. I don't get to tease a billionaire every day."

"Don't worry about it. It's not the worst I've heard. The tea's probably ready. We should go."

I helped her up. She hooked her arm into mine, like it had belonged there for years. We walked down the hall and toward the kitchen.

"You said Fox Silver?"

"Yes, James is the nickname that stuck."

"It suits you. Like James Bond." We both let out a soft chuckle. "But Silver is sexier. James Silver, clever and cunning, diabolical between the sheets."

I quirked an eyebrow.

"Diabolical?"

She wiggled her brows back at me suggestively. "You look like someone who'd have a fetish."

She wasn't wrong. I stopped before we reached the kitchen. Her cheeks were still tinted pink, and her body language, inviting.

I leaned in closer and lifted my hand to her chest, dragging my thumb along her windpipe, then up her neck, until she allowed me to tilt her head into my palm. I lowered to her ear, dragging my lip along its cartridge, and whispered, "You're right. I believe I may have developed a new fetish tonight. And her name is Laura."

She shivered, then stood still. Her body tensed up at my words, but instead of pulling away, she came in closer. Her breath trailed hot against my neck as she whispered back, "I think I may have developed a new fetish too..."

A server arrived with the emergency tea order. "Have it sent to room 209, please. Set it on the coffee table and do not disturb."

"Yes, Mr. Silver."

Laura stood up in a hurry. "I should check on Allie."

I touched her arm gently, to sit back down. "I knew you wouldn't want to hear about the fetish."

She crossed her arms over her chest.

"She's my friend. I need to check on her."

"She's with a doctor."

"What?"

"Julia's a friend of the family and she'll let me know if Allie needs help."

She sat quietly for a moment.

"Thank you for doing that."

"Of course. And now that you're free, join me at the spa. I had a massage booked with my...daughter, but since it's past her bedtime, would you like to come along instead?"

I reached for her hand, guiding her to the hall.

"Isn't it also past your bedtime, sir?"

A laugh bursted out of my lungs.

"The great thing about getting older is not having to worry about such trivial matters as silly bedtimes," I said, walking slightly behind her.

My eyes roved along her curves, drinking in her smooth silhouette. The material of her dress clung to her body like a second skin, and ruffles cascaded down the bodice, creating an ethereal effect. Her chestnut locks shimmered in the light, framing her facial features. A pang of yearning surged through my chest as I gazed upon this woman.

"Fine." She stopped and hooked her arm into mine. "I don't want to catch what Allie has, and a massage sounds amazing, but I still need to check on her."

"Wait—are you two sharing a room?" I asked.

"Of course. We're the nutcrackers, after all."

"You can't stay the night there. It's out of the question."

Her shoulders shook with laughter. "That's impossible. The lodge is full, all the rooms are taken, and the help shares quarters. Plus, food poisoning isn't contagious, and Allie is family to me."

Realizing the difficulty I would face in attempting to persuade her, I exhaled. The elevator took us to the second floor, and I remembered a scene from my mother's favorite chick flick.

The scene where a man corners a woman in an elevator. With one hand, he grabs her wrist and pins it above her head, while with the other, he reaches out and runs his thumb along her lower lip. She stills, eyes closed and chest rising as she waits for his next move. Her gasp is lost in his kiss as he devours her mouth.

I never walked in on my mother watching a chick flick again. But would I play out the scene with Laura? Here? *Fuck, yeah.*

Laura swept her tongue over her lip, bringing my attention back to her face. The jugular vein in her neck pulsed, and it seemed she could barely contain her excitement as we ascended. Once we reached our floor, Laura sped off to her room while I handed her the spare mask I kept in my pocket.

"No condom in there?" she quipped.

"I prefer the warmth of a woman over latex."

A hint of shock raced across her face, but she quickly composed herself.

"Herpes isn't warm either," she said dryly.

Getting a good chuckle at this, I shook my head. "Do you have herpes?"

"No, of course not!"

Relieved, I replied, "Good. Then we don't have a problem."

She set her mask over her face before swiping her card. The sensor pad near the door beeped, and she looked back over her shoulder, saying, "Wait here."

Ignoring her advice, I followed her into the small suite. A fold-out couch was already open with the sheets turned down, where I guessed Laura planned to sleep. She picked up the tea from the table and left for Allie's room. Standing in the doorway, I forgot about the massage appointment I didn't have, and the meeting I promised my cousin to discuss a new organized crime ring. Laura was more entertaining than any boring meeting I could have been stuck in.

"How is Allie?" I asked when she returned.

"She sipped on the tea and fell back asleep. Do I need anything with me?"

"No, you're good. Ready?"

She nodded.

We left the room, and she followed me down a private hallway leading directly to the spa.

"I didn't realize we could go this way."

"I've been coming here since before I could hit on the masseuse." I winked, and she offered a bemused smile.

"This corridor is not on the blueprints."

"The spa is a newer addition with a natural waterfall. You checked the blueprints?"

"Doesn't everyone?"

"No."

"I take it from my overprotective and overbearing parents. I like to know my surroundings; you know, in case the bad guys attack."

I scratched at my jaw. "In case the bad guys attack? You were a nutcracker tonight."

She turned around once she reached the bottom step and set her hands on her hips.

"Sometimes I try to pretend my work is more important than opening doors for billionaires and"—her gaze fell to my crotch—"cracking nuts."

"Ouch." I followed her through the next door.

"So I check blueprints, just in case. You never know when you'll need a quick exit." She stopped at the glass entrance. "It's closed."

I clicked a code on my watch, and the door slid open. Beyond, an oasis of foliage with the sound of a nearby water-fall. The developers built the spa lounge into a pre-existing cave.

I gestured her inside, but she stopped me, keeping her keen eyes on my face. A part of me wanted to force her inside the spa, to impress her, while another was desperate for her to stay right next to me.

"If you're buttering me up for a naked massage, then today may be your lucky day, Mr. Silver."

"I promise, I'll remember that."

"You make promises to women often, Mr. Silver?"

The way my name slid off her tongue made me want to promise her more than the world. I would give her the universe. Anything she wanted to stay at my side, anything she craved—I would make it happen.

"Only to the important ones." I said.

# Chapter 3



He nudged me inside the spa, swaying my attention to a cave illuminated with a bluish hue from the moonlight that streamed in through an opening above.

As a cloud of heat and steam slammed into my body, James lowered his hand to the small of my back, guiding me forward. He did that often, and I liked it.

The lush paradise thrived with exotic plants and flowers, rich in colors and scents. A mountain of jagged rocks towered over the foliage, its surface interwoven with ancient vines and trees. The air was thick with scents of damp moss, rich soil, and earthy plant life, all mixed with the sweet smell of flowers in bloom. Every few moments, the crispness of cool air that wafted from the outside brought back awareness to the magical surroundings. The sound of running water echoed from the cave walls like a waterfall, but I couldn't see one.

"This is one hell of a flex." I turned around to face him.

James was grinning from ear to ear.

"You bring all your dates to this paradise?"

"You're the first."

He spoke with conviction, making each word a promise, and I wanted to trust him. With quiet insistence, he whispered,

"I've never brought anyone here." If he kept saying things like that, maybe I'd be foolish enough to believe him.

"Come on, I want to show you something." He took my hand.

I hadn't held a man's hand before. Not like this. His large, rough fingers intertwined with mine, engulfing my small hand in his warmth. His strength and gentleness held me like an everlasting hug. It felt unfamiliar: like handing over a fragment of my independence but simultaneously getting an immense sense of...belonging.

"It took seven years to complete this project. Everyone in the family had input."

We walked around the corner and came upon the full view of a waterfall. It was a majestic sight to behold; the water was crystal clear and sparkled under the moonlight. The rocks at the bottom were dark and jagged, adding a sense of wildness.

"This is breathtaking," I breathed out, leaning against a railing, completely awestruck, "and it's definitely not on the blueprints."

"I knew you'd appreciate it." James squeezed my hand lightly. "A stream breaks off from the river north of the lodge, and we incorporated the flow into the design."

"Only twenty-five percent of people survive the fall down Niagara."

He laughed. "This is not Niagara, but better. Watch." He walked around the pond's perimeter to the other side of the waterfall. "Can you see me?" he called out over the water's hum.

"No!"

"Okay, now switch places!"

I hurried to take his spot while he took mine. When I did, I couldn't believe James showed through the falling water.

We joined back up in the middle, resting against the railing. Froth broke against the rocks at the bottom.

"It's the optics. At least, that's how the engineer explained it."

A gust of wind rushed through the opening, and I shivered.

"You're cold." James shifted to stand behind me.

I turned in his arms to face him. He curled me into the safety of his embrace, and my heart ached to be closer, still. If only he would kiss me.

"Thank you for showing this to me." I said, lowering my head to his chest. "It's beautiful."

My head rose and fell with his breaths. I felt a lock of hair fall across my forehead, and I absently brushed it back. I listened to the thump of his heart—a bass drum calling out rhythmically from his rib cage. What the heck was happening to me? How on earth did I end up here? The sky poured down moonlight through the large opening overhead, and I yawned.

"You're tired," he whispered, nudging his nose into my hair and inhaling. He did that a lot, and I liked it.

"I had an early morning."

We stood there, embracing until I found my courage to look up and meet his bright eyes. His warmth radiated as hot as his stare. The perfect moment teased me in all the right ways, but he held back.

I tilted my head sideways. "How often do you bring women here?"

"I already told you. You're the first."

"Bullshit."

He laughed. "Why?"

"Because you're a player. Aren't you a player, James Silver?"

"I don't believe so."

My hair kept going into my face, and he brushed it away from my eyes.

"Are you playing me?" I asked.

He saw me as nothing more than another employee he wanted to sleep with. Or at least, I hoped he wanted that. Was this what I wanted? A night of deep, desperate kisses, of hot skin and hungry mouths? Of tracing forearms and palms with my fingertips?

As my body shifted against his powerful frame, a loud, 'Yes,' echoed in my head.

He stroked my cheek with his thumb, and my heart fluttered in my chest. My legs trembled underneath me and I wished I could freeze time.

"You're exhilarating." His low voice stirred the air between us.

"And you're avoiding my question. What's so special about spending time with a nutcracker?"

He tucked his face into my hair again, inhaling deeply. He seemed to absorb me like I was the only thing keeping him alive.

"You see a nutcracker, and I see a sassy, strong, and entertaining woman. Not to mention, absolutely beautiful. You take my breath away, Laura Young."

I liked the way my name rolled off his tongue, and I loved the way he was looking at me with intent, his bright blue eyes dark with desire. My heart pounded in my chest and butterflies fluttered in my stomach. I was breathless as I waited to see if he would finally kiss me. Hooking up with James Silver was not on my Christmas wish list, but how could I say no to the fairytale he created?

He leaned in, his breath hot against my ear. "I have a confession to make," he whispered.

"What is it?" I held the air in my lungs as he towered over me.

"I didn't bring you here just to show you this place," he said, his voice low and seductive.

"Then why am I here?"

My pulse quickened, and my hands shook slightly as I held them around his waist. Blood rushed to my face and body alike, granting me warmth at all of my extremities. My heart thumped with such vigor, there was no way he couldn't feel it against his chest.

"I wanted to be alone with you." Nerves were slowly creeping in, like a vine crawling up a wall, and I wasn't sure what to do.

"Is something wrong?" he asked.

"No," I lied. "I just get in my head sometimes."

"And what is in that head of yours?"

He swept his finger across my forehead. His deep voice oozed with dominance, working its way up my hormone ladder, Bond-style.

"It's kind of hard to think right now," I whispered. "With you. So close."

"Try harder."

His lips twitched ever so slightly, lifting the corner of his mouth. I could barely concentrate. His eyes sparkled with mischief. He definitely knew what he was doing to me and to my body.

"I don't know how I ended up here tonight, with you, but this moment...right now...is all I can think about. It feels...good, right, overwhelming."

"Are you a mind reader, Ms. Young?"

I stared at him in confusion.

"Because I think you're reading my mind."

He gently held my chin with his thumb and forefinger, tilting my face upward to meet his mouth. Our lips touched for a second and a half before he pulled back, leaving me breathless and wanting more.

"Was that out of line?"

The intensity of his whisper sent a chill down my spine.

I cleared my throat. "No, definitely not."

It wasn't enough.

I had the biggest case of breathing blue balls of my life because I couldn't get a breath out. I stepped back.

"Are you all right? You're turning pale."

"Yeah." I heaved in air and lowered my hands on my knees. "I'm. Fine."

"Are you having a panic attack?"

I wasn't sure what it was, but it was definitely something.

"I'm claustrophobic but I don't get panic attacks. Only eleven percent of Americans experience panic attacks, and I'm not in that group." I straightened, and he gripped my wrist with his hand, pressing his thumb over my pulse and observing his watch.

"Your heart rate is up."

"I'm fine." I waved my hand and pushed my shoulders back. "I promise."

He stepped closer and brought me back to his chest, lowering his lips to my ear. "If kissing you softly gives you a panic attack, what's gonna happen when I kiss you like you're truly mine?"

*Oh, God!*

This time, he crushed his mouth against mine, over-whelming my senses by the taste, smell, and feel of him. He wrapped his arms tightly around me, holding my body against his. An electric charge crackled between us, igniting a fire inside me. The warmth of his mouth was intoxicating. His tongue tentatively teased at the seam of my lips, expertly exploring my mouth and dominating with every sweep. His hand cradled the back of my neck, sending tingling sensations down my spine, while his other hand found the small of my back, pulling me impossibly closer. Our bodies pressed together, heat against heat, heartbeat against heartbeat, his erection against my belly. The world, for those few moments, condensed into the space between our lips.

I lifted my arms to wrap around his neck. His hands tangled in my hair, before sweeping down my body, cupping a breast.

If someone walked in on us...

I pulled away, my lips hot and swollen.

"A night with you would be very inappropriate, Mr. Silver. I'm still an employee."

"You're off the clock and alone for Christmas." His lips skimmed mine. "Right?"

I nodded. Technically, I wasn't his employee any longer. And truthfully, a little Christmas fling couldn't hurt anyone.

"So, I must insist you spend Christmas with me and my family."

He gripped me by the hips and brought me close to him again, as if we were a couple. "My parents would kill any of us if we spent Christmas apart. Wouldn't yours?"

I laughed.

"My father will be in the operating room, and my mother is working in her lab on the next cancer cure." I dragged my hands back up around his neck and lifted onto my toes, hovering my lips above his. "But I really don't want to talk about my parents. So, you're definitely single?"

He grasped me by my hips and pulled me in against him. His erection pressed into my belly again, his eyes focused on my lips, and his fingers digging into my skin as he whispered, "Always single."

The power flickered, and he pulled away, robbing me of his lips.

"What was that?" I asked.

"Storms must be near, and hopefully, it's not the computer virus my brother cleared."

"I guess George was wrong about the weather."

"It's the mountains and the changing winds. Electricity goes out at times, but we have generators." He pointed to a maintenance door and checked his watch again. "It's getting late. Let me walk you to your room."

And just like that, the moment between us was gone.

James held my hand, and I followed him like a puppy. God, I wanted so much more than a five minute make-out session. Before I knew it, we were standing at the entrance to his suite.

"This isn't my room," I whispered.

He placed his watch against the plated number on the door, and it opened. We stepped into the extended suite with a tall window lining the back wall. Beyond, night lights illuminated a private swimming pool and a Jacuzzi tub.

I stepped out of my shoes and onto the rug-covered floor of the hallway. The moment my feet touched the carpeting, I knew I'd feel nothing that soft in my life again. The white fibers pressed against my feet felt like freshly spun cotton. To my left, a fireplace carved from a single slab of granite towered two stories high. On the right, double doors opened into a bedroom decorated in warm browns and greens. The place was massive."Earlier, when we were upstairs, you said you were on your way to your room. This suite is nowhere near my room."

"You're observant," he said pointedly, a sheepish smile playing on his lips. "I may have stretched the truth a little. Please, make yourself comfortable."

"You stretched the truth by two floors, a private entrance, an outdoor Jacuzzi, and more." I couldn't get enough of the contemporary country decor. The space oozed warmth and charm.

"If you don't like it, ask the management for a refund," he murmured from behind me.

There was nothing not to like about the exclusive suite. There was definitely a lot to like about the way he held me from behind, rubbing himself over my ass. He nudged his face into my neck, and left a tender kiss, guiding me toward the double doors leading to the bedroom.

A king-sized bed took up most of the space. Monochrome pillows and a matching spread covered the bed. The bathroom was easily big enough to fit fifteen people in it. A fireplace glowed in an alcove on the wall and steam simmered in the air.

"Hmm." I leaned into his hold as he swept his mouth down my shoulder.

"If you continue kissing me like this, I don't think I'll want a refund."

"Good." He let go. A cool breeze replaced his warmth behind me. "But I must apologize. I have to leave for a while."

"What?"

I spun on my heel to face him.

"Business meeting. I have to consult with my partners."

My heart dropped.

"At Christmas?"

"It's one downfall of being a Silver."

"I should head out then."

He shook his head. "No, you're staying here. I don't want you to catch whatever's bugging Allie. I'll check on her before my meeting."

"Will you be long?"

He sighed heavily and his shoulders sagged. "Most likely," he replied, and my enthusiasm plummeted off a cliff.

James leaned in, kissed me on the cheek, and left. I stood in the suite for a few minutes, taking in my surroundings. On the left, glass walls enclosed the tiled shower which was larger than my home bathroom. A ridiculous number of decorative fixtures projected an opulent display of twinkling lights around the ceiling. There was a separate steam shower room and a sauna, both spewing vapor. Two marble sinks adorned the elegant bathroom, offering a touch of luxury. On top of the counters sat lotions, toiletries and scented candles, each set in a beautiful ceramic container that probably cost more than my monthly rent. It had everything I'd ever want, except for a man who came with it all.

I locked the door and plopped on the couch near the double-sided fireplace. Its warmth provided comfort as I gazed out of the large window at the bubbling hot tub. Moments later, the phone rang.

"Hello?" I picked up the receiver.

"Allie's running a fever." James whispered, his voice muffled by a mask. "Julia thinks we should take her to the hospital."

"Oh no! I'm on my way—""

"—Laura, don't. You don't want to catch what she has. We'll make an arrangement for Allie's transfer."

"Thank you. I really appreciate the help."

"Of course. I'll see you in the morning. Good night, Laura."

"Good night, James."

I hung up. The enormous clock on the wall declared I had only six hours until morning, yet I couldn't sleep. I removed my shoes and pulled off my clothes until I was wearing just my bra and panties before grabbing a luxurious robe from the bathroom and tightening it around myself. The outside ther-mometer read a measly thirteen degrees.

"You only live once."

I dashed across the deck barefoot, shedding the robe on my way, and plunged into the steaming hot tub. The roaring jets felt amazing against my sore muscles. I lowered my body until water bubbled up to my chin. Steam rose around me as a party roared somewhere nearby, but I couldn't see anyone. It didn't seem like James would come back, either.

I soaked in the hot tub until warmth penetrated my bones and my fingers shriveled. When I returned inside, I realized all of my clothes were back in my room. I paced to a walk-in closet and dragged my finger over the neatly stacked t-shirts. I picked the one on top, slipping my arms into the enormous holes. The shirt swallowed me. It smelled of expensive cologne and spring. I hadn't realized how cold I'd been until my skin warmed with the cloth's softness. He smelled like home, but he wasn't here.

Tired, I headed to the bedroom and slipped underneath the fluffy covers. They were saturated with his scent, like a torturous drug, reminding me of what could have been. My hand trailed across the soft sheets, and I snuggled into my pillow. I slept without dreaming, but it was one of the most comfortable nights I'd had in a long time.

When I awoke and opened my eyes, I was staring into an identical pair: Kensi's.

# Chapter 4

*James*

Their giggles carried from the bedroom. I set my coffee aside and paced to the door, leaning against the frame.

Laura and Kensi lay sprawled across the bed, moving their legs and arms up and down, their laughter filling the air like the sweetest melody.

My oversized clothes draped over Laura's slender figure, the t-shirt sloping down her shoulders and well past her knees. A heat stirred within me, snaking its way downward as I adjusted my jeans. I longed to undress her, to feel her smooth skin pressed against mine, and to ravish her. But Kensi was here.

I cleared my throat, causing them both to jump. "What's so funny?"

Laura sat up straight and tried to compose herself.

"Look, Daddy! We're making snow angels!" Kensi's arms flapped up and down on the plush duvet.

My skin tingled as I pushed away from the doorframe and crossed the room. I lowered myself onto the bed beside Laura, my eyes tracing the curves of her perky breasts like a starving man at a feast.

"That's great, sweetheart. But we usually make snow angels outside. Go get dressed, Kensi. We'll have breakfast and go make snow angels outside."

"Yay!"

Kensi hopped off the bed and ran across the suite to her room.

"Good morning," Laura tucked a stray lock of hair behind her ear. Her hazel eyes met mine, and a faint blush painted her cheeks.

"Good morning," I leaned in and placed a kiss on her cheek. "I guess you met my daughter."

"Yeah, I guess."

Something passed over her face and I couldn't recognize the look. She seemed...confused.

"What's the matter?" I drew my hand down her shin and wrapped my fingers around her ankle, stroking over her skin.

"You didn't mention a daughter yesterday."

"I never mention Kensi the same day I meet someone."

"And her mom?" she asked, her brows drawing closer.

"We co-parent."

Relief washed over her face, and her mouth slowly curved into a smile. I blinked first.

"Kensi's an amazing little girl." Laura's gaze drifted fondly to the door where Kensi left. "We actually met yesterday in the front lobby. She was excited about the snow, and this morning, she told me everything there is to know about snowflakes. Did you know that no two snowflakes are alike?"

She sat higher on the bed with an enthusiasm I would have expected from Kensi. Except, Laura was a woman. The first woman I'd allowed in my bed since I split with Tiffany five months ago. The first one whose bouncy breasts fucking hypnotized me. I shook my head and lifted my gaze back to hers.

"Kensi has a way of making everything seem new and exciting."

Just like Laura. I didn't tell her that. I didn't want to scare her more than I already had.

I rubbed my hand up and down her shin, and leaned in with a whisper, "Are you ready for some breakfast?"

"Starving."

I placed a tender kiss on her neck. "If you'd like to change out of my t-shirt and into something that won't make me hard, your suitcase is in the closet. Breakfast will be here in ten minutes."

I swear, I saw her nipples harden as I spoke, and my dick twitched in response.

The sight of her aroused body left me with a raging fire in my veins. Every fiber of my being wanted me to reach out, take her, and fuck her. Right there. On my bed.

But she brought herself back into submission, drawing into her own shell before scurrying away like a frightened mouse. "I'll meet you two in the kitchen," she squeaked. I watched her go, still not entirely sure what had just happened.

Ten minutes later, Laura emerged from the bathroom, freshly dressed and looking more than ready to tackle the day. The sight of her joining Kensi and me at the dining table, the snow falling gently outside, felt like a scene straight out of a dream. I was fucking losing my mind over how perfect this seemed.

"Here we go," I said, setting a plate of steaming pancakes in front of the girls. "Hope you like them."

"Thank you," Laura replied, her eyes lighting up as she dug into the fluffy stack. "These are amazing. You're quite the chef."

"Thanks," I grinned. "But I can't accept your compliment. Kensi made these with her grandmother this morning."

"Really?" Laura cut another slice and dipped the piece in

maple syrup. She turned to Kensi. "Did your grandmother teach you how to make these?"

"No." Kensi's eyes widened, and she shook her head so emphatically that her hair, wild from sleeping on it wet, danced around her shoulders. "Mommy and Nana did."

I watched Laura's face, trying to read her mind.

"Well, I'm gonna be honest with you, Kensi. These are the best pancakes I've ever tasted. You're gonna have to invite me for breakfast more often."

Laura gave me a sly smile. Kensi beamed widely, and I was dumbfounded that it took less than twelve hours for this woman to blend into our lives.

As we ate and chatted about everything from skiing this afternoon to Kensi's favorite books, I marveled at how seamlessly Laura fit into our world. The air buzzed with laughter and warmth, a perfect balance of tender moments and light-hearted banter that made me feel more alive than I had in years.

My gaze flickered to the window, transfixed by a flurry of white flakes cascading down upon the world outside. The winds were restless, like a menacing beast lurking at the edge of our abode, and I knew that the perilous weather meant we would soon have to abandon our plans for skiing the icy cliffs.

"How about we build a snowman?" I suggested.

Kensi's face lit up. "Can you come with us, Laura?"

"Of course, sweetie. Let's get bundled up and head outside." Laura's warm voice gave me goosebumps.

We finished breakfast and quickly got dressed in our winter gear, the three of us looking like a trio of colorful marshmallows in our puffy coats and scarves.

Outside, the crisp winter air nipped at our cheeks. Giant flakes drifted lazily from the sky, blanketing the ground in a thick layer of pristine snow. Tall evergreens sparkled with frost, their boughs heavy with ice weight. Nestled in the heart of a picturesque mountain valley, the Silver Resort looked like something straight out of a snow globe.

Laura and Kensi had lain on their backs in the fresh white powder, their arms and legs splayed out wide to make perfect snow angels. The winter sun beamed down, catching all of the tiny snowflakes twinkling around them as if they were diamonds. The image was breathtaking. Despite the frosty air that chilled everything else in sight, these two snow angels sparkled with warmth and hope. For a moment, it seemed like the world was still.

After heading back indoors, I prepared two steaming mugs of hot cocoa with marshmallows, just the way Kensi liked it. When I returned, Kensi sat up in the snow. "Daddy! Guess what? We're snowflake experts now!"

I walked across the deck and set the hot chocolate on a table. "Is that so?"

"Did you know there are one septillion snowflakes in a cubic mile of snow?" Laura quipped, grinning as Kensi's eyes widened.

"Wow, septillion? That's a lot." Kensi hopped up, bouncing on the balls of her feet. She ran up to the table and blew a breath over the steaming mug. "Is that one for me?"

"Sure." I nodded, and she looked up.

"We learned all about fresh snow. Laura's really smart, just like you," she said between breaths.

"Ah," I said. "Well, I think you're pretty smart yourself, kiddo." I tousled her hair before turning my attention back to Laura. Her cheeks were flushed with a winter's kiss. I picked up Laura's mug and carried the hot chocolate toward her. "Stay at the table, Kensi."

As I handed the mug to Laura, she commented, "Oh, you put mini marshmallows?"

"Of course, I did. I'm not a monster."

She laughed, and we both looked over to Kensi, who was

utterly focused on cooling the steaming liquid in her cup with her breath.

"You two have a beautiful connection." Laura's voice was a mixture of awe and disbelief.

"Thanks." Warmth spread through me at her words. "She's the best thing that's ever happened to me."

"But she must look like her beautiful mother because she looks nothing like you."

Keeping Kensi in view, we walked away from the snow angel prints.

"You're right and wrong. I don't know what her biological mother looks like because we adopted Kensi. But she must have been beautiful."

"Been?"

"She died at birth."

"I'm so sorry. That's so sad. Does Kensi know?"

"She's too young, but when the time is right, we'll tell her."

"And Kensi's current mom didn't want to spend Christmas with her?"

Tiffany had her heart set on being with her for the holidays, but it was my turn to have quality time with our beautiful daughter.

"We have an arrangement. Tiffany will spend time with Kensi after the New Year."

"So, no alone time with the nutcracker?" Laura's mouth stretched into a coy smile.

Amid the whirlwind of chaos and laughter that was family life, alone time felt like a fleeting dream. Parenthood of a five-year-old meant that moments of respite were hard won and savored as if they were precious stones.

"Kensi goes to bed at eight thirty and tonight, she's sleeping at her grandparent's."

Laura trailed closer, weaving her free hand around my waist and jutting her hip into my hardening dick, grazing the lust that had been unfurling. Her touch made it even harder to contain a strain of desire that wanted nothing but to be set free.

"Is that an invitation, Mr. Silver?"

I lowered my head to her ear. "That depends. Have you been a good girl or a bad girl this year?"

A sly smirk tugged at her lips as they curved up in an almost feral grin, her eyes glinting with mischief. "I've been a good girl. But I want to be a bad girl tonight, you know, just to see what it's like to be your bad girl."

I rubbed against her hip. "Your wish is my command," I whispered, my tongue running along her ear. She pulled away, nodding to Kensi, who jumped off her seat, and headed our way.

"I finished my hot chocolate. It's snowman time." She clapped.

Another half hour and my daughter would pass out for a nap, giving me alone time with Laura.

"Alright, team," I said, rubbing my hands together. "Let's get to work on this snowman."

Kensi took charge, instructing Laura and me on where to place the snowballs as she supervised. We rolled giant spheres of snow across the yard, each one growing larger and heavier as they picked up layers from the ground.

"His base needs to be bigger!" Kensi was eyeing our progress like a boss. "If he's going to be the best snowman ever, he needs a solid base."

"Roger that, boss." Laura playfully saluted Kensi before getting back to work on the snowman's base.

As we built the snowman together, Kensi and Laura's synchronous laughter rang through the chilly air. In that moment, all my worries melted away, giving me hope this would be the best Christmas ever.

Kensi was in her element, barking orders like a pint-sized

general as Laura and I rolled enormous snowballs across the yard. The snowman's base had finally reached Kensi's exacting standards, leaving us to tackle the midsection.

"You ever think about having more kids?" Laura asked, flashing a smile as we hoisted the second snowball onto the base.

"More little monsters running around?" I feigned horror, chuckling at the thought. "I've considered it, but as you can see, Kensi keeps me on my toes enough as it is."

"Fair enough," she said, brushing snow off her mittens. "But really, I've always wanted a daughter. I mean, I'd be thrilled with a son too, but something about having a little girl... I don't know. It just feels right. Not now, of course. Shit, am I ever not ready for that now, but one day, when the time is right, you know?"

"Sounds like you'd make a great mom," I told her sincerely, watching her eyes light up with warmth. "But if you ever want life to fuck up your plans, don't speak them out loud."

Laura paused, patting the snow to make the ball compact. "I'm on the pill if you're worried. Kids right now are out of the question, but when I watch you and Kensi together, it's hard not to wish for something like that in the future."

"Life has a funny way of surprising us. Kensi was adopted, but she wasn't planned. It was a quick decision, and before I knew it, I was a dad of a newborn baby girl." I gave her a reassuring pat on the shoulder. "What I'm trying to say is, you never know what the future holds."

"Hey, you two!" Kensi called out. "Less talking, more snowman building!"

"Got it, Chief!" Laura shouted back, her earlier melancholy replaced by a playful grin. We sculpted the snowman's torso under Kensi's watchful eye.

I glanced over at Laura, "Life's too short not to take chances, even if they scare the hell out of you. Being a father is the best job I could have, and I wouldn't trade it for anything."

Her eyes sparkled, but her forehead creased with lines of worry. Reading her was like trying to decipher the Enigma machine.

The snowman was complete, a proud sentinel guarding our fledgling igloo. Laura seemed absorbed in adding the final touches—twigs for arms, an old hat, and a crooked carrot nose. Her eyes sparkled with a childlike delight, lifting Kensi's spirits.

"Daddy, I'm going to the bathroom."

"Wash your hands, Kensi."

She ran inside. "I should check on her in a minute, because I'm sure she'll fall asleep on her way back."

Laura set her empty mug of hot chocolate on the table. "Was it more difficult to maintain your relationship with Tiffany after you had Kensi?" Laura asked gently, her hazel eyes filled with curiosity.

"Truth be told," I admitted, "our relationship had already been strained by then. When Kensi arrived, we tried to make it work for her sake, but we just drifted apart. We'll always be committed to raising Kensi together, though."

Laura nodded, her gaze lingering on the igloo we built before the snowman. The snow glistened under the sunlight, casting a soft glow on our cozy creation.

"Would you like to see the inside?" I asked, offering her my hand.

"Sure." She took it without hesitation.

Inside the igloo, the warmth of our bodies tempered the cold air. We sat close together, our breaths mingling in the confined space.

"James," Laura whispered, her eyes locked onto mine, "I want you to know that I think you're an incredible father. The way you care for Kensi... It's inspiring."

"Thank you," I murmured, leaning into her ear. "That means a lot."

"Your love for her is beautiful," she whispered. "If I'm lucky enough to become a parent, I can only hope to be as devoted as you are."

I removed her hat and nestled my nose into her hair, inhaling. She smelled...delicious.

"Something tells me you'd be fantastic, Laura." My voice was barely audible.

The air between us crackled with electricity. We were finally alone, surrounded by snow and silence.

I leaned in and pressed my lips gently against her soft mouth. She tasted like sweet chocolate. Our kiss, tentative at first, deepened with each stroke of my tongue.

"Hey, Dad, look what I made!" Kensi's voice echoed through the igloo.

Our lips parted, and my eyes flew wide open. It wasn't because of Kensi. It was because of Laura—because I'd never felt so intimate with anyone, so connected and fused together. We were two people, but we were also a pair. My heart was beating in time with hers. My breath coincided with the rise and fall of her chest, and our bodies merged as one. But I wanted more. Much more. I wanted Laura.

Kensi came into view, holding a small snow sculpture. "It's a kitty."

"That's incredible, Kensi." The tiny cat resembled a rat, but how could I tell her? "Aren't you tired?"

"Not yet."

I looked over at Laura, who tried to conceal a smirk. Maybe this was for the best because if I took Laura here, we'd melt the igloo.

"Can I put it next to our snowman outside?" She lifted, bouncing on her heels. Where was this energy coming from?

"Of course, sweetheart," I agreed, giving Laura an apologetic smile. "We'll be out in a minute."

"Okay." Kensi scurried out of view, leaving Laura and me alone once more.

"Alone time is difficult to come by when you're a parent, huh?" Laura chuckled, her hazel eyes twinkling with amusement.

"Apparently, so." I sighed, running a hand through my hair. "But I wouldn't trade her for the world."

"Nor should you. She's an incredible little girl."

"She's a little girl who needs a nap, because I have a surprise for you."

"A surprise?"

"Looks like the storm cleared." I pointed to the sky. "Which means, we can go skiing."

Her eyes lit up. "Really?"

I nodded.

We retired from the igloo, and I lifted Kensi into my arms. "It's nap time, sweetheart."

"I don't want to."

"You want to be strong to help grandma cook tomorrow. She's making an apple pie, and she needs your help with the crumble."

Kensi thought for a moment, and hollered, "Race you to the door!" She slid down my body and launched herself with an impressive burst of speed.

"Hey, no fair!" Laura cried playfully, taking off after her, leaving me in their powdery wake.

Kensi declared herself the winner before I reached the door, and she and Laura debated who would've won had they started at the same time.

"Next race," I interjected, wiping snow from my face, "I get a five-second head start."

"Deal!" Kensi agreed immediately, her eyes sparkling with

mischief.

A smirk tugged at Laura's mouth. "You're going to need it," she teased, nudging me with her elbow as we stepped inside.

"Is that a challenge?"

"More like a promise," she shot back, her voice brimming with laughter.

We peeled off our winter gear and settled into the warmth generated by the fire.

"It's time for your nap, Kensi."

"Can Laura tuck me in?" she asked.

"Yes, she can."

I felt the heat of envy and pleasure flood my veins. Their connection made me crave a devoted partner who'd cherish my daughter.

Moments later, Laura pulled me away from my thoughts. "She's asleep. You've been awfully quiet. Everything okay?"

"Fine." I forced a smile. "Just lost in thought, I guess. Come here." I wiggled my finger for her to join me on the couch by the fireplace. She sat beside me and I wrapped my arm around her. "The weather's cleared. My mom will be here in ten minutes to stay with Kensi. We're going skiing.

"Ten minutes? I can do a lot in ten minutes." She ran her hand over my chest and snuggled into my side, laying her head on my chest. I kissed the top of her head.

"What I'd like to do with you requires more than just a few minutes, but the helicopter is ready."

She sat up.

"A helicopter?"

I nodded. "It will drop us off near the summit."

She hopped off the couch and danced in a circle.

"I get to ski!"

She flung herself into my arms, grabbing around my neck as if she were a monkey. My hands found their way beneath her and lifted her so she wrapped her legs around my waist, and I welcomed the feel of her body against mine. Her chest, covered by a sweater I deemed too thick, pressed up against me. Her muscular legs clamped over my hips. With her nails gently scraping across my scalp, an electric arousal passed through my crotch and hardened my dick before I could even register it. A grunt involuntarily escaped my lips.

"I would have offered sooner if I knew this would be your reaction," I quipped.

# Chapter 5

### Laura

His hand over the round ends of my skis and asked, "Freestyle?"

"Sometimes you need to ski backwards." I shrugged.

James zipped up my jacket. I buckled my boots halfway and set a helmet atop my head. "Alright, I'm ready to go."

"Gloves?" He took my hands in his, the touch prompting doubts about this ski trip, because I'd much rather feel him touch me all over.

"Ahem," I cleared my throat, "I prefer mittens. They keep me warmer."

I removed the mittens from my jacket pockets and put them on my hands. "Where's your gear?"

"By the stands. Come on."

We put on our skis and slalomed from the family lodge to an empty helicopter pad. James removed his skis in a hurry and helped me pack mine onto the copter. We climbed in the back and hoisted the headphones onto our heads.

"You aren't flying, Mr. Silver?" I asked.

"Not today, Ms. Young."

He shut the door and secured my seatbelt.

"Wait, I was joking. You can actually fly?"

"I'm a man of many talents." He winked. "So, Ms. Young?

How good of a skier are you? I'll need to tell the pilot where we're headed," I said.

"I can hold my own. Surprise me with what you've got."

"Keep in mind there won't be any help once we reach the summit."

"Don't worry, James. I'm looking forward to it. Take me somewhere with slopes, but avoid moguls—I had a terrible experience last time. I bruised from head to toe, and my ass looked like a rainbow."

He laughed, his broad shoulders bobbing up and down. "I know the perfect spot."

The chopper engine roared to life. The spinning blades forced a chill through the cabin, and my knees jiggled.

"Have you been in a helicopter before?" he asked.

"I flew over the Grand Canyon for my sweet sixteen. It feels like ages ago."

I stared out the window at the view of the valley below. Snow-capped mountains reached into a blue sky. The air was frosty and crisp, and the lodge below looked mesmerizing.

As we ascended higher and higher, I clung to his arm. "If this isn't James Bond whisking me away, I don't know what is! Look that way!" I nodded toward the river behind the lodge. "Is that the stream that feeds the waterfall?"

"That's it."

The pilot turned towards the mountain. The crystal-clear sky made for a picturesque backdrop as snow from the previous night had drifted eastward, dusting the branches of trees. Despite this transformation, the river remained untouched.

I held onto his hand tightly until we landed.

"I can't believe this is happening." The sound of my squeal carried through the valley. We retrieved our gear and avalanche packs, then bundled up. With goggles over my eyes and a mask covering my mouth, I was ready to ski. The helicopter took off, leaving us on top of the mountain.

"Are you ready, Young?"

"Lead the way!"

He dug the ski poles into the snow and let gravity take control. I stayed close behind him an arm's length away, taking a similar route down the mountain. His skiing skills were impressive as he gracefully carved through the pristine powder. He flowed down the mountain with an effortless ease, each turn fluid and precise. The edges of his skis bit into the snow as I glided behind him, shifting my body seamlessly with the mountain's contour.

The steep slope made the terrain challenging, yet it felt like a dance. The shimmering white powder sprayed behind us in a fine mist as we made our descent, creating a mesmerizing trail of crystals caught in the sunlight. Every so often, I would launch off a jump, landing softly and continuing my run without missing a beat. The crisp air held me alert, pushing me to go faster, carve sharper, and challenge myself with each new section of the slope.

The wind pushed against our chests as we raced downhill. Soon enough, my legs were burning with fatigue, and we stopped for a breather at a plateau. The stunning view stretched into the horizon as I took it all in.

"You all right?" He propped his goggles on top of his head.

I removed my face mask and exhaled. A cloud of steam followed in the cold air. "Today is the best day ever! Nothing can top this, Silver. Nothing."

"We'll see about that." He winked.

I wiggled my nose, catching a whiff of smoke.

"Do you smell that?" I asked.

"It's coming from over there." He pointed down the slope. "Come on."

I followed him down the hill toward the smoke. We skied around a row of trees and halted in front of a cave.

I stilled.

I was wrong. I was so, so wrong to think he couldn't top the chopper.

Inside the cave, the walls shimmered with crystalline formations, catching and reflecting the soft glow of countless candles. The warm light revealed a meticulously set table for two, adorned with delicate dishes and sparkling glassware. I gasped, realizing he had orchestrated this magical moment. Every detail, from the echoing drip of melting snow to the gentle flicker of the candle flames, made it an unforgettable moment, a pocket of warmth and romance amidst the cold majesty of the mountain.

"James, this... This is beautiful."

"I hope you didn't think I wanted to get you in bed without a proper date."

I unclipped my boots from the skis, and he did the same.

"A date?" I asked. "This is way more than a date. I... I can't believe you did this."

We set our skis and poles into the snow. He took my hand and led me inside. I couldn't keep my mouth closed. The scene was absolute perfection. He pulled out a bottle of red wine from a cooler and uncorked it with quick precision. The aroma of its dry leaves and plump blackberries filled the cave's air.

"I asked the chef to prepare your favorite meal," he said, pouring red liquid into two glasses. "I hope you're in the mood for steak and mashed potatoes."

"Seriously?," I said, still feeling a bit taken aback by the thoughtfulness. "How did you know?"

"I have my ways, Ms. Young."

He pulled out my chair for me to sit, then took his seat. "Let's eat," he said, raising his glass.

We clinked our glasses together before taking a sip of the

rich and fruity wine. The steak was cooked to perfection, tender, and juicy, and the potatoes were creamy with the right amount of butter. The conversation flowed back and forth, ranging from what we did for a living to our favorite childhood memories. With every passing moment, I found myself drawn to him, intrigued by his tales and amused by his jokes.

He cleared the plates from our dinner, packing them into a backpack, and I realized how much I had forgotten about the rest of the world. For this one moment, all that mattered was the beautiful view of the mountains, the gorgeous man sitting across from me, and the sheer romance of the afternoon. Before I knew it, the candles had burned down low, and we had to leave.

"I don't want this afternoon to end," I whispered.

"It doesn't have to." He replied. "How sore are you?"

I stretched my arms above my head. "A little. The powder was tough."

"We should get going then. I have a surprise for you."

"Another one? What is it?"

"It wouldn't be a surprise if I told you."

I wasn't used to being this spoiled by anyone. "Mr. Silver, if you're trying to get into my pants, you had me the evening we met at the door." I lifted to my toes and placed a gentle kiss on his lips.

A shout echoed down the hill, and I jumped back. Next thing I knew, my boots were fastened and I was on my skis, speeding downhill after a young boy who flapped his arms in the air, crying. He wouldn't make the bend at that speed.

I zipped behind him, widening my stance. I released my ski poles and scooped him underneath his arms. My legs burned from the speed and weight as I hoisted him off the ground. I shifted my weight to the right, turning my skis to stop our momentum. A wall of powder shot out from below the skis.

"Are you okay?" I asked.

"I couldn't stop!" the boy cried.

"It's okay. I've got you. What's your name?"

"Trevor."

"You're Axel Wagner's boy?"

He nodded.

I looked up the hill and saw James approaching, along with whom I assumed was Axel.

"Are you guys all right? You were flying." James stopped just below us, as if securing the hill. I handed Trevor over to his dad.

"Thank you so much. You have my gratitude."

"You're welcome. It looks like the strap broke on the harness, but Trevor managed well on his own." I crouched next to the boy and checked him over before turning back to Axel. "Do you need help to get down the mountain? If you use two ski poles, Trevor can hold on and ski between the legs."

"Yes, thank you. I can manage that. Thanks again."

"No problem at all."

We skied down with Axel and Trevor following closely behind to ensure a safe descent before removing our skis. We set them on a rack near the lobby entrance.

"You call me Bond, but you're the one pulling all the moves, Ms. Young."

I groaned, cracked my neck sideways, and extended my arms over my head. "I think my body will pay for this later."

He held open the front door, gesturing inside. I stopped as soon as I heard the loud chatter by the front counter. Cece and Candy, dressed in snow bunny ski-suits, each tapped a foot with impatience. The receptionist at the desk had a receiver pressed to his ear.

"Crap." James slowly backed outside, and I followed his lead.

"They're looking for you?"

"I've been ditching them since we arrived."

"You can just say no."

"It's not as easy as it looks."

I chuckled.

We scooted across the snow-covered path in our ski boots. The slippery ground forced me to hold on to James for my life.

"Where are we going?" I asked as we slid along.

"We'll use the back way to the spa, through the maintenance room."

We stopped in front of a steel door, and James tapped his watch. The security light flashed, and he twisted the lock open. I followed him inside.

"You're back to being James Bond again!"

"Hold on," he threw his hand forward, stopping me. "Keep this door open while I grab the other one, so we don't get locked out."

"Sure thing."

He unlocked the interior door and waved me over. Moments later, we found ourselves at the waterfall again, looking up.

"So, is the spa closed again?" I laughed, its echo carrying through the space.

"Your laugh…" he started.

"What?" I tilted my head.

The reflection of overhead light danced in his eyes. "It's captivating. Your laugh is like a song. You're captivating."

He inched closer, and I closed my eyes, but I didn't feel the kiss I was expecting. Instead, he bent close to my ear and whispered. "I booked the entire spa, just for us."

His hot breath whispered over my ear, its warmth sweeping through my body. Without another word, he lowered to the ground and removed one of my ski boots, then the other. He hurried out of his own, grabbed my hand, and we headed for the spa.

I showered in the ladies' room, half expecting him to join me, but he didn't, and we met up in the sauna, like we'd agreed.

The sauna's heat hit me like a brick wall, making my skin glisten with sweat. James was sitting on one of the wooden benches, a towel draped over his lap. He gestured for me to sit down next to him, and I obliged, my eyes flickering over his hard, muscular body. He picked up a pitcher of water and poured it over the hot stones. Steam hissed and filled the room. I closed my eyes and breathed in the heat, letting it seep into my pores.

He sat beside me, his towel brushing against my skin, and I opened my eyes, turning his way.

"So, what's next on the agenda?" My voice trembled. Despite my earlier cockiness, I wasn't entirely sure what I was getting myself into.

No. That was a lie. I knew exactly what I was getting myself into.

James grinned. "For now, just relax."

Despite my efforts to heed his advice, my mind was consumed by my greatest desire. Him. Him on top of me. Him inside me. Him all over me. My head spun from the heat until I felt his hand reach across and rest on my knee, and all of my senses zoomed in on the fiery touch. His fingers gently kneaded the skin, higher and closer to my inner thigh. I parted my knees and moaned softly, my eyes fluttering open to look at him. I didn't mean to make the noise, but his touch was torturous.

"You're beautiful," he breathed, his gaze meeting mine. "Do you know that?"

I swallowed, feeling my heart rate quicken.

He leaned in and kissed my cheek, his warm breath trailing down my neck. He stretched across my body, holding me at an angle, and kissed the other side of my face.

I wanted to settle into his touch. I wanted him to kiss me until my lips were raw and swollen. I needed his mouth on my skin and for him to take me like no man had ever taken me before. The thought of being devoured set my body on fire and caused every hair on my neck to stand on end. But I pulled away.

"What's wrong?" He brushed his thumb over my eyebrow.

"I missed my pill yesterday. I... I'm starting a new job in January, and—"

"Condoms work. They're 98% effective."

"The pill is 99% effective. If taken correctly. And since I missed mine yesterday..."

I trailed off and looked into his beautiful blue eyes. He kissed me then, his lips pressing to mine, and I softened beneath his touch. His tongue flicked ever so gently, and I moaned into his mouth. My lower half ached with a burning need.

His hands slid to my shoulders, their pressure forcing me down to the bench. His fingers tickled along my skin as they worked their way down to the sports top—or was it a crop top? —exposing skin inch by inch as he traveled further south. He slipped his finger underneath the towel and my chest lurched forward. The fabric fell off, revealing my breasts. Heat seared from his fingers as they burned a trail around one of my nipples, teasing it with light circles until it hardened under his touch. His fingers pinched it gently, then pinched again, harder, before massaging both breasts with skill. I relaxed against him, gasping for air as his hands moved lower and his mouth traveled across my collarbone. He pushed up against me once again.

"I want you, Laura." His voice was thick with desire.

My head went fuzzy, and I tossed it back, but a stern knock on the sauna door brought me back to the present.

"Mr. Silver, the hot stones are ready."

James groaned.

"Fuck. I forgot about the massage." He paused, looking around the steam room as if trying to find a perfect spot where we could hide. "I'd like to finish what we started, but not here."

"Aha," was the only thing I could utter.

He picked up my towel and wrapped it around me, tucking the ends at my breasts. "Come on. You don't want to miss this."

He opened the door. Cool air slammed into my body, and my legs felt like jelly as we followed the masseuse inside a room with two tables.

The inviting ambiance calmed my nerves. Dim lighting highlighted the silhouettes of strategically placed candles. The air held the gentle aroma of lavender and eucalyptus. Soft instrumental music played in the background, creating a cocoon of serenity that seemed miles away from the bustling world outside.

"Lie face down and cover yourself with a towel."

The massage table, draped in clean, soft linens, beckoned. I settled onto the mattress, unfastened my towel and let it hang loosely over my mid-section. I turned my head to the side and saw James laying on the table beside mine.

"Put your head in the hole. It will be more comfortable."

I nodded and did as he said. When the masseuse placed the first warm stone on my back, an involuntary sigh escaped my lips. The sensation was unlike anything I had ever felt. She added stones until they lined in a column down my spine. I lifted my head and turned to James again. A hot stone rolled down my back.

"Are we getting the same treatment?" I asked.

"We are," he murmured. "But I'm getting the feeling you don't know how to relax."

How could I relax? I was half naked, in a room with a delicious man who spoiled me.

James's voice broke through the silence. "Just let go of all your thoughts, Laura."

I closed my eyes and tried to *relax*. I focused on my

breathing and felt each stone radiating heat on my back, loosening the knots in my muscles. The stones, perfectly heated, felt like miniature suns, their warmth easing the tender ache in my limbs. Each one erased the tensions and worries that had nestled into every nook and cranny of my being.

The therapist's skilled hands moved in tandem with the stones and I drifted into a state of mental quietude. Warmth melted away my worries until there was nothing but blissful stillness left. As she glided them over my skin, the knots and tension in my muscles loosened. The weight and heat drew out the stress, leaving behind tranquility. Now and then, the therapist would replace a stone that had cooled with a freshly warmed one, ensuring a consistent and enveloping warmth throughout the session. Smaller pebbles found their way to my palms, between my toes, and even cradled in the curve of my neck. Each placement felt deliberate, targeted, and immensely soothing.

As she worked her way down, from the nape of my neck, across my shoulders, and down my spine, a sense of complete relaxation took over. Every thought and worry evaporated, replaced by the rhythmic dance of warmth and pressure.

The masseuse removed the stones and began with gentle strokes. Except something didn't add up. Her hands were stronger, the pressure greater and fingers more insistent, and I slowly realized they were James's hands.

# Chapter 6
## James

The spa was a sea of tranquility. Soft music played as my masseuse worked out the kinks in my shoulders, the lemongrass essential oil soothing my senses. Yet, I couldn't settle in.

I lifted my head and turned sideways, catching the masseuse's eye. She backed away at my silent request. I pressed my forefinger to my lips, asking Laura's masseuse to remain quiet. She removed the last few hot stones off Laura's back and left while I took her place.

Laura lay on her front. Her shoulders rose and fell with each calm breath. I let my gaze travel the length of her body, over the lean muscles defining her sun-kissed skin. I poured massage oil into my palms and slid my hands down her neck and to her shoulders, kneading at the tension.

She twitched.

"James?" She tried to sit up, but I pressed down.

"Just relax."

She sucked in a sharp breath but didn't protest. I hid a smile, keeping my touch firm yet unhurried. Her shoulders tensed for a split second before relaxing into my hands. I worked my way down the middle of her back. A soft sound escaped her, not quite a moan, but enough for my groin to tighten. A visible shiver ran through her shaky exhale as she relaxed into the table.

My hands glided along the curve of her spine and around to her sides, rubbing gentle circles over her ribcage. Her skin was soft as silk, warm to the touch. I breathed in the scent of her floral shampoo and something darker, more primal. My mouth watered with the urge to taste her.

Another moan, louder this time. Her hips shifted on the table, thighs parting slightly. I bit back a groan at the sight, heat pooling low in my balls.

My hands drifted to the tense muscles of her ass. Her breath caught—but she didn't tell me to stop. I took it as permission to continue my exploration, stroking along her inner thighs. She trembled under my touch, the soft sounds of pleasure escaping with every breath. My fingers slipped between her legs to find her hot and slick, desire pulsing through her flesh.

She was mine.

"Turn around." I groaned, giving her barely any room to move, but she obeyed, keeping the towel sliding off her body snug as she twisted onto her back.

Moving to the head of the table, I smoothed my thumb down her throat, feeling the strength of her pulse. Quick and irregular. She was nervous. Or maybe excited?

I tenderly ran my fingers along her neck, soothing the delicate area that too often went unnoticed.

"What are you doing?" she asked.

"I'm taking care of you." I cupped her head in my palms and dug my digits into the base of her skull, rubbing circles. Practicing.

She sighed, giving in.

"Good girl."

"We can't—oh!"

*Yes, we can.*

As I worked my way to her collarbone her soft protests

melted into a combination of unintentional yelps and moans. Her back curved and chest lifted. "What if someone comes in? We'll get in trouble."

I laughed at the irrelevant panic in her eyes.

"I won't tell if you won't." I skimmed my fingers along her ribcage, then stopped. "But this is the age of consent, so if you want me to stop, I will."

The question was whether I could. She kept quiet, but her lightly parted lips, flushed cheeks, desperate eyes and erect nipples underneath the thin towel separating us were telling me exactly what I wanted to hear.

"Your body tells me to keep going, my beautiful, but I need to hear it."

She shuddered, desire flickering in her gaze. That's right. I could read her like a book.

"Keep going," she begged. "Please, don't stop."

"Good girl."

I lowered to her collarbone and ran my lips up her neck, ending up at her delicate earlobe."I'm gonna make you feel so good. You'll dream about me for the rest of your life." My lips brushed over her lobe.

She sucked in a quick gasp, and I took over, repeating the trail of kisses down her neck and tasting the palette of her skin. Her nails dug into my arms as I teased her, playing with the towel's edge over her breasts.

"James," she breathed out my name like a prayer. "You're...you're impossible."

"And you're irresistible."

I tugged at the towel's end. It slipped off. Her breath caught in her throat as she lay exposed, her pink nipples standing like bold sentinels against her ivory skin. I circled my finger around her navel, watching goosebumps erupt over her stomach.

Afternoon sun streamed through the transom window,

touching her. She glistened in the massage oil. Her manicured pussy had a landing strip of hair in the center. My blood rushed south as I fought the urge to drop to my knees and worship her between her legs. But first, I'd worship her body.

She lay splayed naked before me, humming with heat as she gripped the sheets at her sides. I rubbed massage oil into my palms, moved to the foot of the massage table, and curved my hands around her shin, pressing my fingers into her calf. She closed her eyes with another moan, and my dick twitched through my tenting towel. It would be so easy to take her.

Instead, I worked her other calf before walking around the table, sliding my hands higher until I reached her thighs, spreading the slick oil over her skin, kneading my fingers deep into the tissue. The higher I moved, the softer she felt.

She smiled, and I kept going—up and down, over the thickness of her thigh, slowly making my way to her hip. I stood mid-way her body, bent low and flicked her nipple with my tongue. A soft whimper escaped her lips, and her eyes flew open, her fingers threading through the back of my hair. I trailed kisses around her erect nipple before tracing the tip with my tongue and sucking it into my mouth.

"Yes." Her ass lifted off the bed and my hand shot out to her hip, holding her down.

She pulled me closer, forcing more of her flesh into my hand and mouth. The towel fell off my hips.

"James..." she breathed.

I cupped both her breasts in my hands, then took a stiff nipple into my mouth while rolling the other between my forefinger and thumb. My ears registered her hoarse cries, urging me on, so I pulled harder while rolling faster as she arched. My dick throbbed, and I lowered my hand down to her pussy, fingers slipping through the lips. I splayed them apart and trailed my fingers over her needy cunt, gathering her essence, pulling upward and gently over her clit.

I lifted my hand to my mouth, getting my first taste of her. She tasted like a puddle of desperation. My fingers returned to her hard little clit, pulling slow circles around the nub, watching her eyes roll back and lips part. Her wanton body bucked beneath my hand. I eased a finger deep inside her tight pussy, and she gasped, back arching off the table as I began the slow, rhythmic strokes.

On the next push, I slid another finger inside her, and pushed them both in, filling her deeply and stretching her tight little hole.

"James." My name on her lips was pure ecstasy, and I wound up the pace. Her inner walls tightened around me as I moved even deeper, discovering the spot that made her world go silent with pleasure. She was slick and ready, her hips rocking in a not-so-subtle plea, and I rubbed my thumb over her clit, ensuring she'd she stars.

I'd fucking make her see them all—just. Not. Yet.

She cried out, one hand flying back to grasp my wrist. But she didn't push me away—she just held on, her grip tightening with every plunge of my fingers. I leaned down to nip at her neck, tasting salt.

Keeping my fingers inside her, I trailed a column of kisses down the valley of her breasts, over her navel and down the landing strip, until my lips found her clit and I flicked my tongue over the spot.

"James!" Her back lifted off the table and her hands flew to my head, urging me for more. "Oh god, don't stop," she gasped.

I lapped at her sweetness. She was close, her inner muscles fluttering around my fingers like the wings of a trapped bird.

I curled them inside her, searching for the spot while I ground my tongue against her clit.

"Please, James." Her eyes flew wide open, and her lips parted with a moan, her breathing broken and ragged. "I need you inside me."

Now, she was ready.

It took great will to pull my fingers out of her sweet pussy. They slid through her folds to prolong her pleasure. I licked my digits, tasting her musky sweetness once more. She was an aphrodisiac that drove me insane. I lifted, looking over her glowing body, and grasped my cock. I stroked twice, lubricating my skin with her juices and my saliva, and shifted back down to the foot of the table. I gripped her ankles and shifted her body until her delectable pussy comfortably met my mouth. I closed my mouth around her flesh, promising a quick release.

"That's it," her voice was a hoarse cry as she wove her fingers through my hair, "right there."

I lapped harder and faster. She rode my face, hips bucking up and down, pushing into my mouth until her legs tensed, muscles trembled and body spasmed in spurts.

Almost there.

I focused on her clit, keeping a steady rhythm of licks, bites and sucks until she cried out in bliss. And then I sucked harder, both fingers pumping in and out of her slippery cunt.

"Come for me, Laura." I murmured against her glistening slit, biting gently on the sweet spot. "Come in my mouth."

My voice was rough with need.

A broken sob escaped her lips, her thighs clamping around my hand to pull me in even deeper. She lifted her pussy and froze in a sea of jitters as the orgasm ripped through her body.

"Ahh!"

She clenched around my fingers, her swollen folds pulsing in my mouth as she shattered, her release spasming in waves. I lapped at her sweet juices, kissing over the tender nub, licking through the aftershocks, over and over, until she gently pushed on my head, and I backed away.

My dick was so hard, it twitched, a drop of pre-cum dripping off the tip.

I needed a condom.

But I couldn't look away for long enough to reach into my robe's pocket. The sun was lowering and cast an orange glow over her goddess-like body. She glistened in sweat and my saliva, beautiful and so fucking irresistible... Forever simply wouldn't be enough. She felt like my beginning and my end.

I climbed onto the bed and spread her legs wide. My cock lay pressed against her belly, sinking into her soft curves as I captured her lips. I dragged my finger along her wet slit again, and she drew back with a moan, "Mmm..."

Staring up at me through half-lidded eyes, she hooked one leg around my ass and pulled me forward. My dick rested between our disengaged limbs, ready to sink deep inside her.

Lights flickered overhead.

I couldn't wait any longer—I had to have her. All of her. She blinked, a soft smile curving her kiss-swollen lips.

"James," she whispered again, reaching for me. "Take me."

A groan tore up my throat as she cupped my face, kissing me hungrily. Could she taste the sweetness of her that lingered in my mouth? Shivers ran down my spine, zapping at the base. Our bodies melded seamlessly from chest to waist as I took over her swollen lips. And the lights went out.

We froze, glued together as one, my cock ready to fuck her brains out. A light tremble somewhere in the valley forced us up on the massage table.

"What was that?" she asked.

"Fuck."

My heart catapulted into my throat. I rolled off the other side of the table in a heartbeat, staggering to my feet as my full balls threw me off balance.

Laura lifted in a hurry, draping a robe over her shoulders as I checked my phone.

"Is everything all right?" Worry creased her forehead and panic flushed her cheeks red.

"Yes, and no. The tremor's from the snow caterpillar. They're gonna smooth out the slopes for tomorrow."

She leaned back against the table. "Thank God. I thought it was an earthquake."

"I thought it was an avalanche." I said.

"Which one's worse?" she asked.

"They're both bad." I said, frowning at the message on my phone. It was from Tiffany.

*Fucking timing.*

"What is it?" she asked.

"I have to go."

"What?"

"I'm so sorry, Laura, but this is urgent." I picked a towel off the floor and wrapped it around my hips. Fucking timing. My ex always had awful timing.

"I should be mad at you," Laura said, tracing a finger down my jaw. "But that was incredible."

I turned my head to press a kiss to her palm. "This isn't over. This was just the appetizer, beautiful"

She bit her lip, and I kissed the inside of her wrist, feeling her pulse flutter. "I'll meet you in our suite. Get in bed and wait for me there. And you better fucking stay naked."

My phone beeped again.

*Fucking Tiffany.*

I headed for the changing room and got dressed in a hurry, cursing under my breath.

When I rushed outside into the frigid night, my body still thrummed with desire, and I was grateful for the cold air to dampen my arousal. Tiffany had called five times in the last ten minutes and texted RED one minute ago.

We had a code. RED meant urgent.

Tiffany answered on the first ring,

"James? I'm so glad you called back."

"What's the emergency?" I asked. It couldn't be our daughter because Kensi was with my parents.

"Just calling to let you know I will make it for Christmas, after all."

"The storm will hit pretty hard overnight, Tiff."

"I know, the worst timing, as usual. My first flight got canceled, but I could rebook."

The wind blew, carrying a cloud of flakes, and the knot in my chest tightened.

"We agreed Kensi would spend the week after the new year with you." I puffed a warm breath into my hands, watching the snow fall. The storm was intensifying, blanketing the world in white.

The phone hummed with static.

"Christmas is not the same without you two," she said.

"Tiff, we agreed—"

"--I know what we agreed to, but things have changed."

*Nothing's changed.*

More static came through the phone. I kicked up a mound of snow. When I picked up Kensi from Tiff's house, my ex was excited to be child-free, so long as no woman came near me.

It was a strange phenomenon: whenever I left the house, Tiff seemed to know. Her uncanny intuition always led her to where I was going and who I was seeing. Laura showed up in my life at the perfect time, and somehow, Tiff got a whiff. Butting into my love life was like her sixth sense.

"The weather's bad." I told her. "You should stay in New York."

"I need to see Kensi and you. I have something to tell you."

Snowflakes melted on my face.

"Stay in New York and wait 'til after New Year. It's too dangerous to fly."

"I can't wait to—" Her voice cut out, replaced by more static.

"Fuck!"

The phone fell out of my hand and slipped into a snowdrift. I picked it off the ground and wiped it dry before heading back inside. Gabe and Hunter sat at the bar, lost in deep discussion. I walked up.

"What are you two so serious about?"

"Check your phone. We just got an avalanche warning." Gabe said.

"Avalanche? I was hoping the storm would halt the planes, not the slopes."

"Winter's a beast this year." Hunter said.

"I see you shook off the twins," I said.

"For now. I shouldn't have brought them. Women are a headache. Period," Hunter replied.

Gabe squeezed Hunter's shoulder, hard enough to make his point. "Says the eighteen-year-old who iced two girls in less than forty-eight hours. Aren't you afraid you'll catch chlamydia?"

Hunter shook his head, saying, "Fuck off. You've got Joanne, and James has a new hook up. What's her name? Laura? I met her by the elevators"

"She's not a hookup, and I have bigger issues," I said with a grunt. "Tiffany's coming for Christmas."

"In this weather?" Gabe asked.

"You know Tiff. If she's after something, not even a storm can stop her."

Gabe removed his phone from his back pocket and swept his finger over the screen. "Which flight is she on? I can have it canceled."

My brother was a genius investigator, bodyguard, and hacker. I forwarded him Tiffany's message, and thirty seconds later, he confirmed, "Done. Tiff will spend Christmas in New York. She'll be pissed, though."

"I'll deal with Tiff when I have to, but I'm glad she won't be here anytime soon. Now seriously, Hunter, what did you do with the twins? I'd like to avoid them if I can."

Hunter poured me a glass of whiskey on the rocks. "They're outside, swimming."

"In this weather?"

"The pool is hot enough."

I took a sip from the glass. The alcohol slid down my throat like honey, warming me from the inside. I tilted the glass further, finishing the drink.

"What's the hurry?" Gabe asked.

"I have a naked woman waiting for me in my bed, so...priorities. I'll see you two tomorrow." I set the glass on the bar, gave each of my brothers a pat on the back, and left for my suite.

An electric thrill zipped up my spine as I swiped the keycard. My heart skipped a beat as I stepped into the room, a lopsided grin stretching across my face, but when I opened the door, the scene in front of me was not what I'd expected.

Rather than seeing Laura lounging naked on the bed, she was curled up on a bean bag near the table. Kensi was tucked into the corner of the couch, her nightgown barely reaching her knees and a blanket half-way off the couch. A pile of toys spilled from the table, including the winter themed puzzles she'd requested for Christmas.

I reached out and tenderly touched her forehead, sinking down next to her. She cuddled into my side, barely opening her eyes, "Hi, Daddy." I brushed the hair off her forehead, feeling a swell of love in my chest.

"Hey, little one," I whispered.

Kensi smiled through her sleep. The sight was so tender and so unexpected that my emotions shifted from predatory to paternal.

"Come on, baby. Let's get you to bed."

I carefully lifted Kensi into my arms and carried her to her room. Laura stirred, lifting off the beanbag.

"You're back."

"I was hoping to find you alone," I whispered. "Hold on."

I placed Kensi on her bed and covered her before returning to Laura. She sat on the edge of my bed, my t-shirt barely covering her thighs.

"Kensi missed you, so your mom brought her by for some games, and then we fell asleep," she said. "She's excited about Santa and she was sure he was coming today."

Kensi's been saying 'today' for a week now, as if Santa would hear her. Laura's leg swayed back and forth in a come hither motion. So I did.

"One more day, and tomorrow the whole family's cooking and getting ready. It's gonna be fun."

I sat on the bed beside her. The mattress dipped underneath my weight, and Laura tipped to my side, looking up.

"Wait, I'm coming?"

"Of course."

I wrapped my arm around her, pulling her close in.

"But it's a family thing."

Her voice quivered. Thankfully, we were seconds away from me shutting her up with my mouth.

"It's a Christmas thing, and everyone joins in." I leaned toward her, my breath softly brushing against her earlobe. "Even the staff. Very casual. Family dinner style."

She shivered in my hold. How could I convince her this was just the beginning?

My feelings for Laura had grown beyond what I'd expected. She was far more than an employee—she'd become someone special. In less than forty-eight hours, she'd become someone I could imagine in our life.

I lowered my mouth to hers when I heard, "Daddy?"

Our lips parted before they even touched. Kensi stood in the doorway, rubbing her eyes. "Can I sleep in your bed tonight?"

I glanced over at Laura who nodded her head in encouragement.

"Of course, darling. Come on up." I lifted her to the king sized bed and placed her in the middle. Laura quietly slid beneath the covers, nestling herself on one side of Kensi, while I slipped in on the other.

Laurs shifted onto her right and propped herself on her elbow, facing the center. "I'm looking forward to tomorrow, then."

I turned my head her way. "Me too."

We stared at one another with Kensi in between us, settling in the gigantic bed like a family, until we both drifted off to sleep.

# Chapter 1



I walked in the bustling kitchen holding Kensi's hand and joined the Silver family around a large marble island. The festive atmosphere immediately assaulted my senses. Red and green decorations adorned every available surface, twinkling fairy lights cast a warm glow, and the scent of gingerbread and mulled wine filled the air. It was like stepping into a Christmas postcard, one that made me feel both nostalgic and giddy. James' mother noticed us first.

"Laura, I'm so happy you could join us."

"Good morning, Grandma." Kensi threw her hands up in the air. Teresa lowered, and Kensi wrapped her arms around her neck, smacking a fat kiss on her cheek. "It's Christmas Eve day, Grandma!"

"Yes, it is. Good morning, sweetheart. How did you sleep?"

"I dreamed about Santa and reindeers and Santa's workers, because they're not done all the work yet and Christmas is almost here. And then I woke up and Laura was there and daddy was there too."

My cheeks heated as I saw Teresa smile.

"Oh, that sounds like the perfect dream and a perfect morning. Go grab a scone and I'll cut it for you."

Kensi went to the table filled with pastries and Teresa turned my way.

"I'm sorry about my son's absence this morning. Those boys of mine are always working."

Maybe it was better that James wasn't here just yet. He'd left early this morning for a meeting with his brothers, which gave me time to process the lengthy orgasm he drew out of me yesterday in the massage room. As incredible as that was. I wanted him to do more. Much more. I wanted him to fuck me silly, until I collapsed, begging for mercy. The memory of his raspy voice, dirty words, and eager fingers seared into my brain. Every time I thought about him on me and inside me, I heated and melted, pooling in my core. We were so close...but always interrupted.

I cleared my throat.

"Thank you for having me this Christmas. I had fun with Kensi this morning. Wow," I breathed, taking in the ambience. "Everything looks gorgeous."

Teresa swept her arm around the room, like she was Mary Poppins who produced the candy cane and mistletoe-themed Christmas. There was so much food everywhere already, the kitchen island overflowing with cakes, healthy snacks and more cakes. "It's not Christmas without a family dinner and all the trimmings."

Kensi returned and tugged on my hand, her eyes wide with excitement as she bounced on her toes. "Laura, do you think Santa will come tonight?"

I crouched down to meet her gaze and gave her a conspiratorial wink. "I heard the winds are high and the storm's slowing him down, but I'm sure he'll make it in time." Her face lit up a sudden surge of affection in my chest. I didn't know how to process my attachment to this little girl, but I liked it.

"Alright, everyone!"

I spun on my heel at the familiar voice as James clapped his hands, drawing attention from the bustling crowd of family and friends. A tight v-neck sweater and fitting pants hugged his muscled body. He looked even better than yesterday, with his freshly trimmed mustache and his hair still damp from a shower. Curls wove through the longer strands.

"Let's get this party started!" someone cheered, and I snapped back to the present.

James continued, "We've got food to cook, games to play, and presents to sort. I checked the app, and it looks like Santa's on schedule to come down the chimney tonight!"

All the kids screamed. It was impossible to not be happy, and I wished Allie were here. I called her last night before I fell asleep by Kensi's side, and she was having her first dinner of solids.

"The responsibility chart hangs on the wall. You all know what to do!"

Another cheer erupted, and suddenly, the room was a flurry of activity. People dashed about, pulling out pots and pans. Hunter and Emma began setting up board games and puzzles on the tables, and Gabe was fixing more twinkling lights above the mantle. The energy was infectious, and despite my initial worry about intruding on the family event, I found myself swept up in their joy.

"Come on." James grabbed my hand. He dragged me toward the stove. "We've got work to do."

He brought out mixing bowls and white powdered sugar, and we began with the Christmas colored icing. Teresa stirred the cookie dough as Kensi kept her eyes locked on the chimney, waiting for Santa's arrival. I fondly thought back to my childhood and the thrill of expecting St. Nick's visit. She was no different, and her enthusiasm was contagious.

"Hey, kiddo," James said, noticing his daughter's distraction. "Why don't you go help Emma set up the cookie decorating station?"

Kensi's face brightened, and she scampered off to Teresa's side. "Come on, grandma. Cookies are in the oven, and we need coconut flakes for the snow."

James caught my eye, and we shared a knowing smile. I couldn't pin what it was about the moment, but it felt right, and I'd learned to trust my gut. Or maybe, it was the magic of Christmas I so desperately craved.

We scooped the icing into glass bowls, and I washed the pots and pans. When I glanced at the chore chart, everyone had claimed a job, so I walked over to the sink and started washing more dishes. As in any kitchen, there were always more dishes to wash.

Meanwhile, James mixed the flour and oats, cutting chunks of butter into the mixture and sneaking glances my way. The twinkling of the Christmas tree lights glinted off his smiling face as he turned to me and said, "Laura, since you're new to our traditions, why don't you be the first to sit on Santa's lap this year?"

I rolled my eyes, trying to suppress a smile. "I'm pretty sure I've outgrown the tradition."

"Ah, but have you really?" he teased, wiggling his eyebrows. "Come on, it'll be fun. We can ask Santa for matching ugly Christmas sweaters."

"Fine," I relented with a laugh, shaking my head. "But what if I have something better to ask for?"

I slowly drifted my gaze down his body, lowering all the way to the counter, which blocked the finest part of him. The low rumble from his chest, which sounded like a warning and a promise, centered in my core.

"Deal." He chuckled and turned his attention back to the stove.

Teresa hastened into the kitchen, her arms laden with an assortment of colorful candy decorations. Kensi trailed behind her, her eyes wide with excitement as she took in the sweets.

She set some chocolate treats on the counter for Kensi, who hopped onto the stool and began sorting through the goodies.

"Do you need help with those?" I asked Teresa.

"Sure. Thank you."

I left Kensi with James in the kitchen and joined Teresa in hanging chocolate bonbons all around the Christmas tree.

"Christmas is always a production when my boys are working. And don't get me started on Hunter and those two girls. He's on a break with Grace. She's not here this Christmas, but you'd like her."

"They seem to follow the chart well." I nodded to the fireplace where Hunter and Tristan were setting up space for something... I wasn't sure what it was, but it included a stage, lots of lights and poinsettias, and an enormous red chair, trimmed in gold rope.

"True. If there was no chart, there would be no Christmas." Her eyes widened, and her smile grew comical.

"And this bonbon tradition?" I asked.

"That comes from our grandparents. When I was young, we hung apples, walnuts, cookies and oranges. Then times got better and one day my grandfather brought home a bag of chocolate bonbons to add to the Christmas tree. It's been a tradition ever since. To better times."

We each unwrapped a bonbon and popped them in our mouths. The velvety taste of rum and raisins overpowered the chocolate with an aromatic flavor that lingered on the tongue. It started off sweet, then slowly transitioned into a hint of smokiness from the dark rum, finishing with a slight tartness from the raisins.

"These are delicious." I left some coco on my tongue to cherish the taste longer. Teresa picked up an oval sweet.

"The chocolate barrels have alcohol. Hang those up high so the kids can't reach."

I stepped up on a stool and followed her direction.

"James mentioned he was with someone new, but I didn't realize it was you," she said.

"Is that a good thing or a bad thing?"

"It's a good thing. He's never been lucky in love, and Hunter's not helping by hiring the escorts." She carefully spaced out the chocolates hanging on the tree, then moved onto the cookies.

*Love?*

"Oh, we're just friends." I said.

Teresa froze in the middle of lifting her arm and lowered her hands on her hips. She scanned me over from top to bottom and gave me a pointed look.

"Don't give me that 'just friends' talk, Ms. Young. Cindy and Karl Young would call my son a great catch.".

She caught me off guard.

"You know my parents?" I asked.

She smiled.

"Your father saved my husband's life. He's an incredible surgeon."

"Thank you," I replied, removing the items from the cart. "He is."

I didn't know my dad operated on Mr. Silver, but then again, my father never mentioned his patients.

"My son has had his share of frivolous girlfriends, but between us, he deserves someone talented and driven. Someone like you."

I fidgeted. Was she trying to set us up? I had no time for a relationship while policing the streets. But I ached for something more than fleeting moments of pleasure. Something longer-lasting and meaningful—though what that meant was still unclear. How long had it been since I'd opened myself up like this? Too long to remember, much less admit.

"So...you're saying James is really single?"

"Yes, and he's adamant it will stay that way."

My heart sank a little, and I'm not sure why.

"But you could change that," she said.

My head snapped up.

"You can't make someone want something."

"What if they don't know whether they want it?" Teresa lifted a brow.

All right. So she was trying to set us up.

"James is an adult. He should know what he wants."

She puffed out a fresh laugh and stepped down the ladder. "The Silver men don't know what they want until it stares them in the face. I should know - I have three sons and four brothers, all of them private detectives. It takes a special woman to fill their lives."

Was she suggesting I was the right woman for him? I was up for a fling, but that's where my fantasies about James Silver stopped. Right between the sheets. All right, I'll admit it. Maybe I wanted more than a fling - like a couple of flings, or maybe a few more?

I sighed, because deep down, I knew I could never get enough. Not after what he'd done to me yesterday. And the way he looked at me guaranteed all sorts of feelings each time.

I peeked from behind the Christmas tree, looking for Kensi. She was sticking her face up the unlit chimney, checking for Santa. "And Kensi's mom is not the right woman?" I asked.

"Tiffany? They're good co-parents and awful partners, so that makes it a no."

"Did they...did they end on bad terms?" I asked, curiosity getting the better of me.

Teresa set the stepping stool against the wall. "They realized they weren't good together. Tiffany's an interior decorator and she can be...difficult. And James can be...difficult in his own ways. But they both love Kensi, and that's what matters most."

Difficult, huh? That didn't sound promising.

"Come on, Kensi, it's time for the finishing touches at the cookie station."

She waved over at her granddaughter to join us by the window.

As we set out scoops of sugary glaze and confetti-colored glitter, Teresa told me about James and his siblings, painting a vivid portrait of a spirited yet unified family.

"Sounds like James was quite the handful," I said.

"Ha!" Teresa snorted. "That's an understatement. By the time he was four, James was climbing trees, furniture and walls. He broke his arm on the swings one year, then his left wrist snapped when he claimed he could jump off the roof. I don't even know how he got there, but when he set his mind to something, nothing could stop him. He was always a good kid at heart. And now he's grown into a wonderful father."

Once we'd finished setting up the station, I helped Kensi wash the soot off her face, and she fell asleep on the couch. Tristan lit the fireplace, where we sat with cups of tea. It was only one o'clock, and the house already smelled like Christmas.

"Is the family always this excited about Santa?" I asked.

"Every year, and it never gets old."

I leaned in closer and lowered my voice. "And who plays Santa?"

Teresa winked. "Ah, now that's a secret."

I snuck a sidelong glance at James as he playfully joked with his brothers. He'd make the perfect Santa.

He stood in the middle of the room, a goofy grin playing on his lips. His family went back and forth between him and each other, their conversations punctuated by loud laughter, until he appeared at my side with a teasing grin.

"Excuse me, ladies. There's a crisis in the kitchen. We've run out of cinnamon for the eggnog, and I could use an extra pair of hands. Laura, care to join me?"

He took my hand before I replied, forcing me to my feet. I

waved back at Teresa with a guilty look, my cheeks burning and insides melting.

"You need help with cinnamon?" I asked.

We zigzagged through the crowd; me following him like a sheep. He was making it so obvious that he was on a mission, and the further away we walked, the more nervous I became.

"That was an excuse." He said as we turned the corner. He pulled me into the pantry and closed the door behind us.

"That was a lousy excuse, but now that we're here, I'd better find cinnamon."

My fingers flew from shelf to shelf, as if I didn't hear him, but then his arms grasped my waist and he spun me around. His touch was electric, magnified by his meaningful hold as I pressed against the wall of his chest. He held me in his arms with my breasts squished between us. His thumb grazed over my chin, tilting me upward so that our eyes could meet.

"You tasted like honey and salted caramel yesterday, Ms. Young," he whispered, his breath hot on my lips and his dick hard against my belly. I squeezed my thighs together as if that would stop the sudden discomfort in my panties. His eyes flicked down to my mouth before returning to meet mine. "What do you taste like today?"

He licked gently over my mouth and my lower parts suddenly remembered how good the pull of his tongue had felt down below. Not that I'd forgotten. How could I?

"Chocolate and rum," he murmured. "Did my mother give you a bonbon?"

"She did."

"Good choice, but I need to finish what we started in that spa," he said.

My heart started racing as I held his gaze, caught in the spell of his bright blue eyes that twinkled with tiny silver stars.

"But we're in the pantry." I whispered, like that would stop him. He seized my mouth, and all I could get out was a gasp that twisted into a desperate moan. I wrapped my arms around his neck and sank into the kiss, melting my body into his. I craved someone like him. Someone who could help me forget about the past, someone who could fill the aching void in my heart and someone I could share my deepest secrets with. Someone who'd lift the burden of guilt and show me how to live once more.

I was so close to having what he had—a family, with a daughter of my own. But one ghastly night, they took it all away. Every nerve-endings in my body came alive as I realized that, maybe, I wanted more than a fling. Maybe I wanted everything I'd lost. I chuckled through the kiss and he pulled away. "What's so funny?"

"Nothing," I lied and pressed my mouth back to his, because how could I tell him about all the feelings bubbling up inside me, and me wanting so much more with him than I'd thought, before we even slept together. All right. So, he'd gotten me off with his strumming fingers and vicious mouth. He'd devoured me, and he'd made the entire day about me and his daughter. But was that enough?

We broke apart for air, and James rested his forehead against mine, panting. "Penny for your thoughts," he said.

I chuckled again. "I don't think you can afford this one, Mr. Bond."

"Try me," he said. "I've seen a lot in my brief life."

I couldn't. "I don't know. It's just... This is one of the best Christmases I've had in my life."

"That makes me very happy, Laura."

I liked how he switched between my last and first names. It was like a game. And now, we were on a first name basis again.

"I can't stop thinking about kissing you." His voice was rough with desire. "All the time."

His hand ran up my skirt, and my thighs parted. I smiled

against his mouth, gently biting his lip. "Well, you're definitely a good kisser."

He went in for my lips, but this time I playfully pushed him away. "I'd love to stay in here with you all night, and have you ruin me some more, but someone can come in at any moment, and we have a party to attend." I reminded him.

He thought for a moment, then gave me that sly and predatory look.

"Meet me in the attic in fifteen minutes."

"What?"

"I know you can find the attic, since you studied the blueprints."

"Yes, I know where the attic is."

The pantry door opened, and Kensi walked in, her lips smeared with chocolate. James quickly removed his hand from underneath my skirt.

"What are you two doing in here? I need help with my Christmas list for Santa."

"We're looking for cinnamon. There it is." I grabbed a random bottle from the shelf and walked out of the pantry, embarrassed, as if Kensi had caught me with my hand in a cookie jar.

"Come, Kensi, let's check that list right now." I heard behind me and glanced over my shoulder just as James lifted his daughter into his arms. My heart melted. I never thought I'd find the look so sexy.

Kensi and James went off to check her list, and I hurried to the powder room to freshen up, my lips swollen and tingling as if he were still kissing me. When I arrived at the attic with two minutes to spare, James was already there.

# Chapter 8

### James

The attic was dimly lit, filled with old chests and forgotten treasures. A thin sheen of dust covered the dated furniture, and shadows lingered in the corners. I found comfort in the simplicity, but felt let down by the lack of luxury. Laura deserved better.

She showed up with two minutes to spare, lips swollen and glowing in the dim light. The slanting beams of evening light filtered through the window, casting a gentle glow on her face.

"Romantic and old," she quipped. "Just the way I like my men."

I laughed through the thick air. I wasn't sure what it was about dusty attics, but they had their charm.

"You came," I said. What a stupid thing to say, but fuck, I was nervous. Like a boy who was about to lose his virginity again. She stepped closer, her eyes twinkling in the dim light, and I caught her floral scent. It mixed with a sugary vanilla I smelled on her breath, like she'd had another bonbon.

"Come closer. I won't bite too hard today."

She closed the distance between us like a cougar. As if she were the one hunting.

"I liked the way you bit me. And I liked the way you sucked on me. But this is what I want today."

Her hand slid to my dick, fingers curving over the fabric at my crotch, rubbing over my shaft. She was on the prowl.

"You want my dick?"

She lifted on her toes and whispered in my ear. "That's correct, Mr. Silver. I want your dick in my mouth and at my mercy."

Her tongue followed the curve of my ear as she lowered, and a rough growl vibrated through my chest.

I tilted her chin higher. "Baby, you've got this all wrong. Once my cock is in your mouth, I'm the driver."

Her breath hitched. She gave me a coy smile and slipped her hand down my pants so unexpectedly; I hadn't even noticed when she'd unfastened my zipper. She reached into my boxers and locked her fingers around my cock, saying, "We'll see."

Her icy hand colliding with my heated skin made my breath get stuck in my lungs. Her touch was torturous, and I pressed my lips against hers to take over. I kissed her hard and with need until her limbs softened and her body melted into mine. She let go of my dick and wrapped her arms around me, her hands roaming over my back and nails gently scraping where my hairline met the neck.

"You're a vixen," I whispered, flicking my tongue over the tip of her earlobe before trailing kisses down the side of her neck and up again to take her mouth all over. As I pulled and sucked on her lips, they met my need every time, demanding proper care. I bit at her bottom lip, not hard enough for pain, but with intention; and she pulled away, breathing hard.

Behind her, light streamed in from the single attic window like a ribbon.

"James," she whispered, my name hanging in the air between us, heavy with longing.

I backed her against a post. My mouth went for her neck again, like a fucking vampire, tongue sweeping over her heated skin. I held both of her wrists above her head with my left hand while caressing her hipbone with my right. I pushed into her soft body, my erection pressing right into her stomach. A small squeak escaped her lips, which I smothered. Kissing her would never grow old.

I pulled my mouth away from hers, trailing my tongue over her bottom lip, and returned to her ear. "This is gonna end with me between your legs."

She looked up. Her eyes sparked with mischief as she reached for my belt and tugged it hard, freeing the leather from its loops and loosening my pants at the same time.

*Fuck me.*

"I don't think so, Mr. Silver." She winked, spun us around, and backed me against the post. My back pressed to the wooden column, and she yanked my pants off my hips. My erection sprang free, and her focus shifted completely to my cock. She grasped me with her cold fingers, and I let go of a guttural groan as she lowered to her knees.

"Laura..."

My hands immediately found her head, fingers weaving into the bouncy curls as she traced her tongue lightly over my crown and teased along the sensitive underside.

"Fuck," I breathed, bucking my hips and involuntarily pressing myself deeper into her mouth. She swept her tongue down my length, stretched her jaw, and took me all the way to the back of her throat before sliding off and making sweet love to my cock with her mouth.

"Fuck, Laura—" I groaned harder, my breathing ragged and erratic. My fingers tangled in her hair with impatience, urging her to take me deeper and faster. She struggled for less than a minute before working her lips and tongue up and down my cock like she couldn't get enough. But I needed more. As if hearing my request, she cupped my balls in her free hand and pressed her finger underneath them. A long thread of a current flew from the base and up my shaft. I bumped the back of my head against the post, harder.

"Laura…"

I gripped her throat in my hand and popped out of her mouth. She held her mouth wide open, ready and willing, and this time, I slid my cock slowly in, watching her face before retreating, her saliva shining in the dim light. In and out. In and out. I placed both of my hands on each side of her face and held her steady so I could fuck her warm mouth at my pace, quick and shallow strokes in between deep thrusts. She obliged and looked so beautiful on her knees. First, pleasure zapped through my balls, spreading down to the base of my shaft, up again until it almost reached the tip. Heat radiated from my skin as she panted and moaned, as I dragged her head back and forth over my cock.

Her body trembled slightly. I could tell she was enjoying herself, but I lost it when she paused. I popped out of her mouth again, and she looked up. Her eyes filled with lust as she reached between her legs and dragged her fingers over her cunt before licking them and taking me back into her mouth.

*Fuck me.*

I could almost taste her essence, and I could definitely smell her excitement. When her full attention returned to my cock, she spared no mercy. She braced her hands against my thighs for support and bopped her head up and down, but it was the sounds she made that undid me. The orgasm zapped through me, and I spilled in her mouth. She sucked me dry and slowed to slower strokes until I was drained.

My cock still pulsed inside her mouth as she looked up at me with a lazy smile playing at the corner of her lips.

"You taste like sweet heaven," she said quietly before lifting to her feet.

*Me?*

But I had no chance to ask as the sound of Kensi's voice reached me from the door. "Daddy?"

We froze.

Panic flooded my veins, and Laura's eyes glossed over with pure horror. I watched her swallow the remaining cum in her mouth.

"Shit!" I pulled up my pants, failing miserably. My hands were shaking uncontrollably, and my fucking heart was about to fly out of my throat.

"Daddy, are you in here?" Kensi called out again.

My daughter had the timing of a rusted clock. Thank God, the post behind me was wide enough and the room dark enough to keep us both from view. I finally tucked myself in and zipped up in a hurry. It wasn't easy with a hard on.

"We can't let her see Santa's sack. It's full of presents," I said.

"That's the sack you're worried about?" she hissed, pulling her sleeve over her mouth to wipe it dry.

"I'm coming, Kensi. Wait by the door. It's dark in here."

She grabbed my hand and pointed to my tented crotch. "You can't go like that."

"I don't have a choice," I gritted.

"Will it down."

"It doesn't work that way."

Laura straightened my shirt and stepped out first, saying, "The chimney is clear for Santa. We're coming, Kensi!"

"You checked the chimney?" Kensi called back, louder this time.

Laura glanced back over her shoulder. "Find something to cover yourself with."

I brushed the dust off my shirt, grabbed the first thing I found, and hurried to the door with a ball of yarn at my crotch.

"Hey, Kensi. We checked the chimney, and it's all clear for Santa." My voice shook like I was fifteen again, on my way to lose my virginity to my hand for the thousandth time. But Laura's mouth was so much better, and her pussy, fuck... I had to stop thinking about her pussy, or the yarn wouldn't help. *And why the fuck did I choose a ball of yarn, anyway?*

"What's on your chin?" Kensi pointed at Laura, who quickly wiped herself. "It looks like eggnog."

"Grandma gave Laura one of her special bonbons," I explained.

*Jesus, why was I bringing my mother into this moment?*

"I think some of it dripped on my chin, but the chimney's clear and ready for Santa. Let's go downstairs."

Laura reached for Kensi's hand, for which I was grateful, as it gave my dick time to settle, but Kensi was a curious child.

"What's that?" she asked, pointing to my crotch.

"It's yarn for Laura. She's gonna make a scarf."

"You know how to crochet?" Kensi's attention returned to Laura. "Grandma knows how to crochet."

And there was my mother again.

"Laura has a lot of talents none of us knew about."

The skin over her bare arms flashed a rosy pink as she glanced back over her shoulder, throwing me a look of guilt.

"Come on, sweetheart. Let's wash our hands and find your grandmother. I feel like I could use a few more of her special bonbons."

They walked ahead, hand in hand, while I contemplated how to prevent Kensi from telling my mother she'd found us in the attic, checking chimneys and sharing secret eggnog.

Laura took Kensi back to the family room, and I stole the opportunity to wash myself and change into a pair of pants that weren't stained with my cum. When I returned to the room, I found Laura sitting by the bar. I ripped off a branch of mistletoe and headed her way.

I tilted Laura's stool back . Her legs flew up and she yelped.

I held the green branch over our heads and sealed her mouth with an upside down kiss. Her lips gave into mine, soft and welcoming. She tasted like eggnog and spiced rum. Our lips parted with a smack, and I glanced over at the bar with two empty glasses.

"You taste delicious."

She giggled, composing herself.

"So did you. Almost like...eggnog, but not quite."

*Fuck.*

I burst out a laugh and pointed to the bar.

"How many of those have you had, Ms. Young?"

"I wasn't counting, but your family keeps on giving me these drinks..."

She gestured with her hand to the row of glasses I hadn't noticed on her other side.

As if on cue, Hunter returned to the bar. He instantly replaced Laura's nearly empty glass with a full one.

"Hey, that's enough for her." I warned, but Laura had already put the drink to her mouth.

"Relax, Silver. They're not strong, and I know exactly how much I can take." She winked.

"You heard the lady," Hunter said. "She knows exactly how much she can take."

"Aren't you supposed to be with Cece and Candy?"

He checked his watch. "They left an hour ago. The next storm wave, as per weather report, will start in two and a half hours."

"Does this mean you'll be hanging out with Laura now?" I asked, giving him a look to fuck off. Instead, he smirked, like pissing me off on Christmas eve was the best gift he could get.

"I don't know. That depends on what the lady desires."

"She desires for you to get the fuck out." I pushed gently on his shoulder. Thankfully, Hunter left with a chuckle.

"Hey, don't be so mean to your brother." She accused, slightly swaying on the chair before taking another sip.

"You know, he looks like a younger version of you."

"Who?"

"Your brother. Were you also a big flirt?"

"I hope not. Wait, was he flirting with you?"

"Does it matter if he was when his older brother is the one I want?"

"Good answer, Ms. Young, though next time, no more drinks from Hunter." I removed the one she held in her hand and set it far away on the bar. "He makes them stronger than you think."

A light burp escaped her tiny mouth, reminding me of her swollen lips around my cock.

"Excuse me." She covered her mouth.

I shifted in my seat and wove the mistletoe into her hair in the same way I tied daisies into Kensi's braids.

"Now I can kiss you over and over," I told her, and she shivered.

She still had her mouth covered when she said, "I don't know. I'm not feeling so well."

"Are you gonna barf?"

"No, I'm not gonna barf. I'm not that far gone yet, but you're right, Hunter's drinks are to die for... I mean, they're murderous... No, they're fucking killers." She giggled.

I liked her dirty mouth more than her drunk one. She then added, "Don't worry, Kensi's playing with Trevor, and they set up the cookies and milk for Santa.

There was only a single cookie I cared about tonight, and it definitely topped Santa's.

"Will you sober up in time for Christmas eve dinner?"

"What?" Her head snapped up, brows narrowed, and she made the same confused face as Kensi when she was reviewing her addition.

"I thought that was tomorrow."

"Yes, Christmas day dinner is tomorrow. Christmas eve, is tonight."

"Jesus Christ, this is the longest day of my life. And is Santa coming today?"

I laughed. "Yes, Santa's coming today."

If Santa got it right, he'd come more than once.

"Kensi will be sleeping at her grandparent's again, so I can have you all to myself."

"Sounds like the perfect gift for us both," she replied, sipping on a fresh drink. I hadn't noticed when she ordered the cocktail. "But I have no gift for you."

"I can think of a few things you can give me tonight. If you're sober."

"It's eggnog and coconut rum, so it's almost like a meal. Your dad said it's the best combination."

I shook my head. "Oh, Ms. Young, it appears my family's ruined you."

Her lips turned up in a wide smile, and she tilted her head. I tried to read the sly look on her face, but I wasn't ready for her reply. "And you? When will you ruin me?"

'Now' was the appropriate reply, but someone mentioned dinner in fifteen minutes.

"You'd better sober up before Santa comes tonight. You don't want to be on his naughty list."

She leaned in. "We both know it's too late for me, unless you call what we did in the attic not naughty enough?"

She was playing with the fire that ignited in my dick.

"Oh, Ms. Young, I have so much to teach you."

A few minutes later, everyone was gathering for dinner. She hopped off the stool, and I caught her by the elbow, leading the way to the long, rustic dining table, laden with a potluck-style feast that would rival any royal banquet. Each dish had a story to tell, from Aunt Marge's legendary green bean casserole to the mouthwatering venison stew whipped up by one of the chefs on staff. Candles flickered in the dimly lit room, casting a warm glow. The scent of pine and cinnamon filled the air while laughter rang out in harmony.

Kensi sat across from me, beside Laura, her tiny legs swinging back and forth. She admired the twinkling lights above head, lifted her hand and pointed a finger, counting the bulbs.

"One, two, three..." I tuned out her voice and connected my gaze with Laura's. She looked absolutely stunning. Her hair was tied up with loose strands hanging here and there. The up-do exposed her long neck, reminding me of where my lips had roamed over her skin. I couldn't keep my eyes off of her. Every time she caught me looking, she would smile and bite her bottom lip, driving me wild. A twitch triggered in my pants. I wanted this woman like I'd never wanted another before.

"Can I have your attention, please?" my father boomed, his voice somehow cutting through the conversation and clinking tableware. My uncle stood beside him, both silver-haired patriarchs beaming with pride as they surveyed the room until it was finally quiet.

"First off," my father began, "we want to thank all of you for joining us in celebrating another fantastic year here at the Silver Lodge. Your hard work and dedication have made Silver Brothers Securities what it is today—an unstoppable force."

"Here, here!" Tristan's dad chimed in, raising his glass in a toast. "We couldn't be prouder of our sons and their growing empire. And let's not forget the amazing team behind them"—he gestured to the other employees—"without whom, none of this would be possible."

"Right you are, my brother," my father continued. "It's been a year of growth for all of us. We've expanded our services and reached new heights, all while maintaining the high standards we set for ourselves. So, grab a glass and raise it to the future of Silver Brothers Securities!"

"Cheers!" everyone chorused, raising their glasses in a toast.

"Cheers," I echoed, lifting my glass—looking right at Laura, who sipped on a darker shade of eggnog.

"Is that with rum again?" I asked her.

"It is. Why?"

I saw my brother chuckling under his breath. Hunter was fucking enjoying this like the spoiled brat he was. Inconsiderate prick.

"Because I need you sober tonight," I lowered my voice.

"It's just a little spiced eggnog. Hunter makes them perfectly. Right Hunter?" She bumped her shoulder against my brother's, who sat on her other side, lifted her glass to her lips, and winked like a devious vixen.

"Right," he replied.

"Are you trying to get her drunk?" I asked him.

"A lady's glass should never be empty."

"It's all right, James. I can hold my own. I promise, I'm fine. Besides, I'm not driving home."

I poured a glass of water and passed it to her. She seemed to converse well during dinner, helped Kensi with her portions, and answered all of my daughter's questions about Santa, and she had three glasses of water before we finished dessert.

"Okay, everybody! It's time for the annual Christmas skit." My cousin Emma stood up from the table and started gathering the family by the fireplace. Kensi had her own part this year, and she hurried after her aunt.

"Come on, Young, I saved you a spot with the best view."

I walked around the table, snaked my hand around her waist and led her to the comfortable lounge by the other fireplace. The spot had the perfect view of the skit. A group of kids, ranging in age from six to twelve, filed onto the makeshift stage.

Laura settled in, and I leaned in to kiss her cheek. "I'm sorry, but I need to leave for a bit."

"You're not watching?" she asked.

I checked the time. "I can't. I have a prior engagement."

"Oh, come on, Silver. It's Christmas Eve."

Exactly. It was Christmas Eve, and Santa had a job to do.

# Chapter 9

*Laura*

December twenty-fourth was officially the longest and most confusing day of my life. It was also a day I would never forget, for all the right and wrong reasons.

I changed my spot from the armchair near the fireplace to the barstool and took another swig of Hunter's special. The alcohol rushed through my veins, setting me on alert and on fire, close to overheated winter jacket strength, border-lining hell. I couldn't believe James left, just like that, in the middle of his daughter's performance. I swigged harder, taking in the buzz that soothed my soul.

Until then, tonight was one of the best nights of my life. The intimate family dinner we'd shared, the good wishes we'd exchanged, and all the wonderful stories I'd heard from Kensi about her dad filled me with all the Christmas joy I could contain. The evening would have been better if he'd stayed.

Emma stepped forward as the narrator. Her infectious enthusiasm brought an instant smile to my face.

"Once upon a time, in the magical land of Snowflake Valley..."

Tuning her out, I convinced myself the warmth in my chest wasn't related to the chocolate rum eggnog in my hand.

Julia stopped by and clinked her glass with mine. "I see you're as interested in this as I am. Merry Christmas."

"Merry Christmas. Did you hear anything from Allie? She didn't answer my texts."

"Turns out she had salmonella, but she's stable. Sleeping a lot."

"What?"

"She's in good hands, but she'll need a few weeks to recover."

"Okay. I guess that's good. Thanks for checking in on her," I said.

"Of course. Let me know if I can help," she said before leaving to be with her boyfriend.

The family room was crowded with family and friends—the Silver brothers, their cousins, parents, and the Wagners filled the couches right by the fireplace. Handmade paper snowflakes suspended from the ceiling by thread, floated in the air. Lights wrapped around windows and beams, and evergreen branches decorated the mantel with ribbons and ornaments.

The room carried the scent of pine and cinnamon. The Silvers laughed and embraced, their cheeks rosy from the warmth of the fire and the subtle buzz of spiked eggnog. There were so many of them. The kids finally finished their skit and happily waited for Santa's arrival by the Christmas tree.

Hunter removed the empty glass from my hand. Seconds later, someone handed me a new one. The brothers talked about skiing and safety as I sipped on my drink. When I'd finished half of the cup, and the eggnog had finally made its way to my bladder, I politely excused myself to the bathroom. I freshened up and when I returned to the group, Emma came up and tugged on my arm. "Are you looking for James?"

"Yes."

She let out a short giggle.

"What's so funny?"

Emma covered her mouth with one hand and gestured to the lounge entrance with the other, where an effervescent Santa Claus stood with a red sack of presents hanging over his shoulder.

"Is that him?"

The noise died down and Emma rushed closer to the hearth near Santa's chair, where James was sporting a complete costume, including a silver beard, silver hair and a faux belly he gripped with pride.

The plush red suit was trimmed with luxurious white fur, and a matching hat sat atop his head. The bushy white beard and mustache completely obscured his face, but his piercing blue eyes still shone through, adding intensity to the jolly character.

In his other hand, he gripped the handle of a prop lantern, wrapped in a candy cane pattern. It cast a warm, flickering glow over the scene.

"Ho, Ho Ho!" he bellowed, his voice an impressively deep rumble. "Merry Christmas!"

The adults chuckled, impressed by his commitment, while the children squealed and rushed around. Kensi stood a few feet away, eying the man as if he were an intruder, and I wondered whether she recognized him. But once the silver Santa distributed gifts to the eager children, he won Kensi over in a heartbeat.

He seemed nervous, but barely showed it. As he interacted with each child, I caught glimpses of the real James—the charming, attentive man who genuinely cared for those around him. The one likely concerned about the drink in my hand.

"Ho, ho, ho!" he bellowed through the room.

I perched on one of the taller stools in the back, and as he handed out the first gifts, I listened to James' aunt and uncle read the nativity story. More eggnog was served, carols played overhead, and a family-like atmosphere enveloped me all over again. They shared nostalgic memories and silly jokes. Each member of the family told Santa what they hoped for, and every few minutes, James glanced in my direction, though his voluminous white eyebrows blocked his vision.

The grandfather clock in the corner chimed nine o'clock and Santa's duties were far from over.

"Alright folks, gather round!" James bellowed, his voice muffled by the bushy white beard. "Santa's got a few more tricks up his sleeve tonight!"

A hush fell over the room as everyone turned to watch him. His eyes scanned the crowd, searching for something or someone, and I couldn't help but feel a flutter in my chest when his gaze lingered on me for a moment longer than necessary. He quickly snapped back into character, raising his hands with a flourish.

"First, we have a special treat for our younger guests, and it rhymes with... chocolate!" he announced, reaching into his seemingly bottomless sack. "But before that–" he paused, shooting me a knowing grin, "–can someone fetch me another drink? This suit is hotter than the devil's sauna."

Everyone laughed.

"Coming right up, Santa." Aunt Marge disappeared into the kitchen. Moments later, she emerged with an absurdly large mug of what I assumed was rum and coke, which she handed him with a sly smile. "I'm hoping this will get me off your naughty list."

"Oh, Aunt Marge, we all know that's impossible," James replied, tipping an imaginary hat in her direction before downing the beverage.

Everyone laughed again.

As James continued to hand out gifts, his eyes occasionally met mine, sparking a connection that sent shivers down my spine. The room's warmth and rum in my veins surpassed cozy pillows and clouds.

I was nursing a fresh drink from Mr. Silver when Emma grabbed my arm. I resisted the pull until I noticed everyone's attention on me.

"It's your turn," she said.

The room fell silent.

I looked at her, puzzled. "My turn for what?"

Santa gestured for me to approach with one finger. The corners of his eyes crinkled up as he gave me a knowing smile. The play of light and shadow on his face drew me into his spell like no other experience I had known before or have since. Though I could not see him clearly beneath his beard and thick brows, I felt his gaze intently locked on my body.

"It's your turn to sit on Santa's lap." She waved me over, ensuring the entire room focused on me. "Don't be shy now."

I set my drink aside before slipping off the barstool and standing up. The buzz of both alcohol and nerves coursed through my veins like a boiling river as I made my way towards Santa's throne. I could feel the heat in my cheeks and my palms were sweating. Despite my shaking I managed to cross the room, fully aware of all eyes on me.

My throat felt dry as I said, "Hello, Santa."

Someone in the crowd shouted, "Sit on his lap!", so James took hold of me and swung me around by the hips. He lowered me onto his lap before I could react and held me so inappropriately close, I worried the kids would get the wrong idea.

"I forgive you," I whispered.

"For what?"

"For leaving me earlier without an explanation."

"I was hoping the Santa Suit would explain itself." His breath whipped through my hair as he whispered, "By the way, you look insanely hot. Hunter can't stop staring at you."

I tugged on his beard and replied playfully, "What about you, Santa? What are you looking at?"

"Everything but you," he said.

I quickly pulled back. "What?"

He tightened his grip on my hip and mumbled, "When I stare at you, I get hard. And since I have children sitting on my lap, I can't allow that to happen."

I playfully wiggled my bottom on his solid thigh and let my leg brush over the arousal pressed against his Santa trousers. He wasn't lying about the hard on. "What do you plan to do about that?"

He looked around the room like searching for an exit, then rubbed his hand against the crotch of his pants as he stared at me with hooded eyes.

"Obviously, Santa will need a bathroom break. Want to join him?"

"Don't I get to tell you my wish first, Santa?"

He stilled as I wiggled my behind.

"Stop fucking doing that, or I will lose it." Despite the warning, a slow smile built on his face. "What is it that Santa can do for you this Christmas, Ms. Young?"

I barely said anything, yet I was out of breath. But he'd had his appetizer in the sauna and I'd had mine in the attic. It was time to plan the main course. I hesitated before leaning in. I covered the side of our faces, in case someone could read lips, and whispered, "I'd like to be your personal gift this week."

His low chuckle set off vibrations along my skin and his hot breath fanned over my neck as his grip tightened over my hip. "And what does that entail, Ms. Young? Because I don't want, nor do I need, a hooker."

"That's not what I meant."

"All right. Explain. What does this personal gift entail?"

Thankfully, his normally booming voice was low enough that only I could hear. I leaned closer again, this time brushing my lips over his earlobe. "I want you to unwrap me slowly."

A grunt rumbled through his chest, and his hand slid up my sweater to cup my breast. I don't know how he did it out of sight, but he did. And when he pinched my nipple, I nearly jumped off his lap. "Consider it done, Ms. Young."

He released me from his hold, and I stood up, wobbling, of course, because who the fuck pinches your nipple in the middle of a family event? His gaze burned deep into my back as I walked away. I glanced over my shoulder and bit my lip as James covered his crotch with an enormous gift.

"Alright, everyone! It's almost time for Santa to leave. Let's sing another carol!"

James clapped his hands to rally the crowd and started off with Rudolph the Red-Nosed Reindeer. I joined the others in song, my mind abuzz with thoughts of what had just transpired and everything I wanted to transpire, and before I knew it, I lost track of him.

The magical atmosphere that seemed to draw me closer to a man whom I'd only considered a fling was contagious. Maybe it was time to accept he could be more than a fling?

A couple of drinks later, plus a personal lap dance with Santa, and my panties were hyped up like Christmas lights.

"It's time for Monopoly and Twister!" someone announced when we'd finished singing.

Axel stopped by with a drink and clinked his glass against mine. "Merry Christmas, Laura."

"Merry Christmas, Axel." I sipped. "How's Trevor doing?"

"He's bragging to his grandparents about skiing faster than his father."

I chuckled softly, my laughter barely audible but crackling with warmth. It must have been the eggnog.

"There's little fear when you're young." I said.

"Thank you for your help on the hills. I got an unexpected call, and the harness snapped—"

"Don't mention it. He probably gave his mom a fright when he told her what happened."

"Chloe's not around anymore. She passed away a few years ago."

I clasped my arms around my middle. "Oh, that was insensitive of me. I just assumed since twenty percent of couples are single-parent households…"

"No harm done."

"Still, I'm sorry."

"Thank you. We won't be venturing up the hills tomorrow. A snowstorm's on its way. Stay inside."

"I will."

He left, and I waited for James to return. How long did it take to change from a Santa's suit?

Kensi found me rummaging in the kitchen fridge for a snack.

"Are you hungry too?" she asked me.

"A little."

I needed carbs to soak up the alcohol in my stomach.

"Isn't it past your bedtime?" I asked.

"There's no bedtime today. Tonight is a special night. And I'm waiting for a call from mommy."

She fiddled with a phone in her hand. "You have a cell phone?"

"I told you. I'm waiting for a call from mommy but the storm outside is stopping the signal. That's what uncle Julian said. And now, I don't know if mommy will call because I miss her and I want her to come, but there's a lot of snow."

"Oh, Kensi. I'm sure your mommy misses you as well, but it would be too dangerous to travel now."

"I know. That's why I want her to call. I have to tell her about our snow angels, and the igloo and Santa."

"Don't worry, baby. I'm sure she'll call before the day is over."

"Thank you." She hugged my waist. "I had fun today."

My heart expanded, knowing I had made little Kensi's

holiday special. If there was one person I had hoped to make happy, it was her. "Did you?"

"Yes," she said with a nod. "And you know what else?"

I shook my head. "What else?"

She bit her lip and looked down like her wish wasn't supposed to be mentioned. "I touched Santa's beard, and he smiled, and then he lifted me up on his lap! He smelled of cookies and candy canes." She giggled, then sighed dreamily, sitting on a kitchen stool. "I can't wait until Christmas morning because the stockings are still empty, so Santa has work to do, and when the stockings overflow, he puts the presents under the tree, but some presents can't fit there because some presents aren't fiscal."

"Fiscal?"

"Yes, like when you wish for grandpa's health and he gets well, that's not a fiscal gift."

I ruffled the top of her hair. "You mean a physical gift?"

"Yes."

"Is that the kind of gift you'd like?"

"Yes. I want mommy and daddy and you for Christmas. So we're together, like a family. And then we can build a snowman family."

"Oh, Kensi." I sighed. "Has anyone ever told you that you have a special heart?"

"I have a special heart and a special kidney," she said.

"What?"

"That's what mommy says. She said she would call before Santa came and..."

Kensi's phone rang, and we both jumped, startled.

"It's her!" She hopped off the kitchen stool.

"Pick it up," I urged.

She slid her finger across the screen and smiled from ear to ear. "Hi, Mommy."

I watched as she scurried off to the bean bags by the

window and sank into one of them; her face was radiant with a smile wider than I'd seen it all day. She loved her parents so much. If life could pause and remove the stress and pressures, growing up wouldn't be so hard. I grew up fast, but I had no choice. At the time I needed my parents' love and support most, I couldn't find it.

And what I needed now was a stronger drink.

# Chapter 10
### James

I removed my Santa costume in a hurry and stepped into the shower for a quick rinse. My tux for the evening hung, crisp, in the closet. I put on a fresh shirt and flicked on the television. Airlines had canceled all flights, so Tiff wouldn't show. Thank god. The woman clawed her way into my life a decade ago when Silver Securities updated its interior design. We worked great in the beginning... Until we didn't. I adjusted the bowtie and smiled to myself: tonight was all about Laura.

I found her at the bar, holding a drink. The low-cut dress showed off her ample cleavage, while the short hemline revealed her toned thighs and evoked an immediate sin in my mind. She crossed one leg over the other, covering the appetizer I couldn't stop thinking about.

Julia left Laura's side, and I walked over to the bar.

"A martini, shaken, not stirred."

She slowly spun around to face me, holding back a chuckle.

"You're sitting underneath a mistletoe, Ms. Young," I chuckled as I brandished the festive sprig of greenery I had stolen from the lobby. Obeying an instinctive impulse, I swooped down to capture her mouth in a kiss before she could react. Her lips were warm and pliant beneath mine, tasting like need and rich alcoholic beverages. I pulled away with reluctance.

"The mistletoe in my hair is no longer enough? You know, you don't need an excuse to kiss me."

"That's good to know." I lowered my mouth to hers again for another smooch and asked against her mouth. "How are you feeling?"

"I have a lot of feelings today, but I know I'm not drunk."

"Good girl."

She shivered. "You clean up well, Santa."

She lowered her hand to my chest and circled her palm over the fabric of my tux. "Wow. That's…snug." Then she grabbed my pectoral muscle and gave it a playful squeeze.

My eyebrows flew up. "Are you okay?"

She hopped off the chair and almost stumbled. I held her steady by her elbow.

"Yes, sorry… You're a hot Santa and an even hotter taxman," she said with a flirtatious smile.

"Taxman?"

"Tuxedo, tax-man."

*Oh, no.*

"How many of those have you had?" I pointed to the glass with the melting ice cubes inside.

"It's not my fault. Your family just loves eggnog—especially the kind with rum."

"And how many eggnogs with rum did you have?"

She showed half-an inch distance between her fingers and whispered, "I think a bit too many. Shh!"

Her forefinger pressed to the middle of my lips, squishing my mouth. I captured her hand in mine and kissed it. "My family has ruined you, Ms. Young."

She gave me a half drunken smile. "Maybe it's because you're taking your sweet time?"

I ran my hands through my hair, struggling to keep myself

from pulling it out. The solution was obvious. Despite her drinking, I wanted to ruin her now, but that wasn't in my nature. I motioned to the server. "A glass of water, please."

He filled a glass and passed it her way.

"Drink."

She drank a quarter of the content before I figured hydration wouldn't be quick enough. The night was slowly ending. Julian sat by the fireplace with Kendra, scrolling through his phone, and Hunter was probably whacking off all his mistakes back in his room.

I said good night to my parents and Kensi, then returned to Laura and took her underneath my arm. She wobbled all the way to my suite. When we arrived in the bedroom, she plopped on the bed like a beached seal. I unzipped the golden dress. It slid off her beautifully toned body with ease. A feather tattoo marked the ribcage underneath her breast with the words *She Believed She Could, So She Did.'*

By then, my erection was at full mast, but she wasn't even conscious. I covered her with a blanket, before heading to the bathroom, where I stepped underneath a cold shower to ease the throbbing in my groin. The shower didn't help. I adjusted the tap to warm and grabbed myself. My need pulsed with each slow stroke. My vision of Laura's body spread over my bed and her pussy in front of my face—like she'd promised—came to mind. With each stroke, I imagined the feel of her skin underneath my fingertips, and with each thrust into my hand, I felt the sensation of her tight heat around me as I finally sank into her.

My strokes sped up, and my breaths grew shallow. I turned to face the wall, bracing one arm against it. My muscles tensed as I imagined my hands on her body. I'd savor the taste of her skin and the feel of her breasts. And I'd watch as her nipples changed their shape, hardening underneath my touch. Warmth surged down my spine and out of my dick. My balls zapped with spasms, and I let out a guttural moan, pushing hard into my fist, and coming heavily.

My pulse quickened as I stood beneath the shower's pounding water. I closed my eyes and remembered Laura's mouth on me, her torturous touch and how she took me in between her beautiful lips. A craving, an insatiable longing that threatened to consume me, stirred. But I didn't want to come again. Not without her. Next time I spilled, it would be inside her.

With a sigh, I reluctantly stepped out of the shower and found a pair of fresh boxer briefs. I walked to the living room, where I poured myself a glass of whiskey from the decanter. It felt like fire coursing down my throat and did little to dampen the cravings pulsing through my veins. Memories of our time together filled my mind and sent shivers up my spine. When I had her again, it would be pure fireworks.

I finished the drink and turned towards the bedroom door. My heart pounded as I waited for any sign that she was awake and ready for me. But there was only silence. I went inside anyway.

Laura lay in bed like a sleeping angel, the blankets pulled tight around her lithe frame. I stilled at the sight of her. She stirred faintly, her breaths soft and slow. I sat beside her, my heart thudding as I dared not to wake her. With tenderness, I laid a whisper-soft kiss on her skin, my mouth barely brushing against her temple. I left her in my bed and reluctantly walked away to the sofa.

SHE OPENED her eyes at half-past nine the next morning with a groan, "Ouch."

"Tylenol's on the nightstand, and I'll bring you coffee."

She quickly sat up as if something was wrong. "Oh, my God, what happened? Did we?"

I stood up and walked over to her bedside. She watched my every step, eyes wide and lips slightly parted. I sat on the bed's edge and lowered to kiss her cracked lips, whispering. "You would have remembered if I'd fucked you."

Her cheeks tinted a pink, and she covered her mouth with her hand, mumbling, "Morning breath."

I handed her a pill and a glass of water.

"Coffee's almost ready, and I ordered breakfast," I told her.

She ran her hands through her hair in confusion.

"What was in that eggnog?" she asked.

"Rum. A lot of rum, according to my great-grandpa's recipe. You don't remember when I warned you?"

She shook her head. "I need a hot shower and a change of clothes, for sure."

She scanned the surrounding area, and I cleared my throat.

"They shut down the ski lifts. There's an avalanche warning, which means we have a stay-in day ahead."

"Where's Kensi?" she asked.

"Probably in the kitchen, eating breakfast with her grandparents."

"So we're all alone?"

"Correct."

"And you're telling me I passed out and ruined our night?"

"Did you have a good time yesterday?" I asked.

"Yes."

"Then you didn't ruin anything, and I assure you, today will be better. After you shower off that eggnog and rum."

She swatted me with a pillow, hopped off the bed and left for the washroom. I arranged breakfast by the fireplace. It was snowing again, with little visibility.

Not long after, croissants, pastries, and other treats arrived. The smell of freshly brewed coffee permeated the room. Laura changed into a pair of leggings and a fluffy sweater before sitting at the table, ready to eat. "I'm so hungry!"

So was I.

"You, put your Santa hat on." She pointed, and I obliged.

"Is that better? If I recall, Santa has a gift to unwrap this morning."

She searched her memory, her eyes finally lighting up. "It's good to know Santa keeps his promises."

I stared at her from across the table as she savoured the pancakes, her lips begging to be kissed. I couldn't help but imagine how she would feel and look writhing beneath me, her soft body succumbing to mine. The more time passed, the more vivid my plan became, and as breakfast ended, I reached across the table and took her hand in mine, pulling her toward me. She looked up with a mix of surprise and desire.

Without a word, I pushed the chair back and stood up. I picked her up and placed her on the table's top, scattering plates and cutlery aside.

"James, what are you doing?"

"If you have to ask, I'm not doing a good job."

I dove for her mouth. My hands roamed over her body as I kissed her, my fingers trailing down her waist and underneath her sweater, her small gasps in my mouth singing like an invitation.

Her sweet taste and the fresh smell of shampoo consumed me. I kissed her hard, like I could lose everything she offered in a moment, but when I lowered over her body, the table trembled. I set my palms flat on the top and waited as the ground shook underneath us. Laura's eyes grew wide. She gripped my arms, fingers digging into my skin.

"Did you feel that?" she asked.

The ground quaked again, and we hurried off the table. We stood underneath a door frame until the shaking stopped.

"What was that?" she asked nervously.

Stress gripped at my neck. "Three possibilities: an earthquake, an avalanche, or worst-case scenario, an earthquake and an avalanche."

"Awesome, but not comforting."

"Hang on."

I grabbed the binoculars and focused them on the mountain, but with the heavy snow and zero visibility, all I saw was white. The lights flickered in and out, and moments later, my phone started ringing.

I swept my finger over the screen.

"Gabe?"

My cell phone beeped, its battery was almost dead.

"Is everyone okay? Wait, I'll call you right back. I need to check on Kensi."

I hung up the phone, and dialed my mother.

"We're okay; everyone's okay," she said when she picked up.

The lights flickered again.

"We'll likely lose power, but the generators will kick in when we do. How's Kensi?"

"Worried the quake caused damage to the chimney and Santa couldn't come down with the stocking gifts last night."

"The gifts are already there, but stay in your room until we check for damage."

"James?"

"Yes, mom."

"You realize, your father, my brothers, and my sons are all calling me worried at the same time? Gabe's on the other line."

"That's because we *are* worried. Tell him to hang up. I'm calling him back."

As I dialed my brother's number, the power went out. I paced between the window and the table. "It looks like the generators aren't kicking in, and my phone is running out of juice. I'll check the maintenance room, and you head to the reserve bunker," I told him.

"Got it."

I hung up and dropped my shoulders.

"You have to leave?" Laura hunched over.

"Just to the maintenance room. It won't take long."

She chewed at her lip. "Don't billionaires have staff for this?"

I smiled knowingly. "They do, except on Christmas day when everyone wants to spend time with their families."

Her somber mood lifted as fast as it fell, and she hopped off the table. "I'm going with you, Bond. This could be fun."

"All I have to do is flick a switch."

"Excellent!" She clapped and ran to the door, where she slipped on her shoes. "I'd love to watch you flick a switch." She laughed.

I gave in. "All right. Come on."

We wound our way down the hallway to the spa, illuminated only by the light streaming from the water hole overhead. Snow had surged over the tiles.

"Watch your step. It's slippery," I said.

The sound of running water reverberated through the space. When we reached the maintenance room, a sweet aroma of flowers and mint drifted through before I took out my pocket-sized keyring and opened the door manually.

The lock clicked, and we slipped into the dark room. Laura jumped as the door closed behind us.

"We're locked out."

I turned on the flashlight and reassured her with my hand on her arm. "Don't worry, I've got the key. Stay here and touch nothing."

I squeezed between two rows of shelves to the end of the room before finding the generator switch. A current revved up the engine, and the lights came on.

Across the brightened room, Laura's face lit up.

"Told you I could flick a switch."

She immediately went back to the door to open it, but found it locked.

"Hold on," I told her as I made my way back. I attempted to open the door by twisting the key in the keyhole, but it was stuck.

Laura fidgeted, tapping her foot and looking at me like we were on the brink of a war. "Open the door already!"

"I'm trying. I seriously can't. It feels jammed." I twisted the key back and forth, adding a little too much force on my eighth try, and the key broke.

*Fuck.*

She stumbled back into the counter behind her, her eyes wide and full of panic. "Why are you doing this to me?"

Her lips paled.

"I'm sorry, I'm not trying to keep you here." I said. "Are you feeling alright?"

"I'm… I'm claustrophobic," she shot back, her voice laced with fear. Her face fell ashen, and her eyes clouded over. I watched as her breaths quickened. I shook my head in disbelief.

"I did *not* know you're claustrophobic."

She glared at me, tears on the brink of spilling from her eyes. "Of course, you knew! I told you the day we met! You know everything about me. You're my boss, for God's sake, and I'm sure you do background checks, and your family knows my family, so no wonder, we finally bumped into one another, and now… Now, we're going to die together in this room."

Her quiet breaths turned into hasty pants as she clutched the counter for balance.

I tried to remember but only had a vague recollection of her briefly mentioning it when I asked if she was having a panic attack. To be honest, I assumed she was embellishing something that made her uncomfortable. Whatever the case, this was serious, and I needed to handle it quickly. "Hey, hey, hey.

You're alright. Let me call my brother to open the door from the outside."

I tried to reach for my phone, but it was lifeless.

"Damnit!"

"What's wrong?"

"My battery died. Do you have yours?"

"No."

I barely heard her weak reply.

"Are we really stuck here?"

The tears that welled in her eyes spilled over, and her lip trembled. I grabbed her face between my hands and kissed her so deeply, she wouldn't be able to think about anything else. Her body instantly gave into my hold as I caressed her mouth with gentle tongue strokes and brushed her lips with soft kisses. I pushed away her fears until her tension drained and her body softened.

She stood up on her toes, wrapping her fingers around the back of my neck. Soft whimpers escaped from her throat. I ran my palms along her waist before tracing them up to cup her ass. But just as I did, she pulled away, breathless.

She looked at me, then at the door, unsure which way to go. Eventually, a small smile crept over her lips before she guided my hand underneath her sweater and onto her bare skin. My finger brushed over a sensitive nipple. She held her breath and my stare, testing my self-control. I had none. Not anymore, and not right now.

"Nearly eight billion people live on this planet, and I get the honor of being stuck with you. What are the odds of that?" I asked.

She swallowed hard and whispered. "One in eight billion… Perhaps, a bit less."

I pinched her nipple, and she jumped with a whimper, searching my eyes for more.

My mouth twisted sideways. "I'm ready to unwrap my present."

I edged closer, giving her little space to breathe. She held herself up against the counter as my hand slipped from her chest and down to her torso. Her eyes widened, and my dick pulsed harder. I slowly roved my fingertips past the elastic waistline and into her perfectly manicured pussy.

I gently parted her with my fingers, feeling her arousal as I ran them through her wetness. She closed her eyes, breathing hard and shivering beneath my touch. Her head rolled back as her breath hitched. My thumb moved in slow circles over her clit. I kissed her neck, my hand working her pussy.

She moaned, her body arching into mine.

"James…" she whispered. "Please… "

I leaned in close, my lips brushing her earlobe.

"I love it when you beg, beautiful. It's time to sit on Santa's face."

# Chapter 11

## Laura

The room heated. Sweat dripped down my back, and when I swallowed, it felt like a pit passed through my throat. We were stuck in a room with limited air supply, and James's mouth was distracting me.

He lifted me onto the counter, yanking my pants down and burying his face between my thighs. I cried out, tangling my fingers in his hair as he licked and sucked, his tongue exploring every inch of my flesh. He was moving so fast, the thought of the contained room nearly vanished. I moaned to the tune of his tongue strokes. He teased my thighs with kisses before returning to my pussy, giving me no time to breathe. I threw my head back, surrendering to the pleasure. Every inch of me trembled underneath his mouth, but I needed more. I wanted him inside me. I needed him to fuck me, hard.

I writhed on the counter but gently pulled him up to his feet and I kissed his wet lips, tasting myself on his mouth. I gripped his ripped arms, holding on for my life. He swallowed my whimpers before trailing kisses along my jawline and to my ear. He did that a lot. And I liked it.

"I need you on the floor, sitting up here," he pointed to his face.

My pussy throbbed.

"I want you inside me."

"Soon, beautiful. But first, you come in my mouth."

His chest rumbled and my pussy leaked. He stood in front of me, while I sat butt naked on the counter with my knees hugging his waist. I leaned in, pressed my mouth to his, and fumbled with the band of his jogging pants. How stupid was it for me to drink last night and miss out on everything that could have been?

He removed my hand for the second time and grasped the hem of my sweater, lifting it above my head. Braless, my breasts sprang free in front of his face. He leaned in slowly, keeping his gaze on my breasts. I watched as he trailed a column of kisses down my chest and to my breast, clamping his mouth around one nipple, and teasing the rim. My other breast was lost in his hand. My head lolled back, and I shivered as his hot breath and slick tongue danced over my chest.

James let go of the tender nipple and skimmed a downward path between my breasts before pulling back. He looked me up and down, his eyes turning a darker shade of desire.

He moved lower, still caressing and licking every inch of my flesh. His hands cupped my buttocks, gripping them tightly as his mouth explored. I clung to his back, trembling at the shooting sensations when he licked around my navel. He chuckled against my skin before planting a hundred tiny kisses across one side of my hip bone. I reached for his waistband, but he stopped me.

"Not yet. Santa needs your pussy bursting in his mouth."

He looked so damn cute in that hat. Wait, what? Fuck. If he kept talking like that, my pussy would burst on its own.

"I want more than that." I lowered my hand to his dick. "I want—"

"My dick?" he asked.

The huskiness of his voice made him even cuter.

I nodded. "All of you."

"I'll give you everything you want"—his sly grin stretched across his face—"after my breakfast. No more interruptions."

He removed the leggings from my ankles and parted my knees, exposing me. Cool air collided with my heated skin, but James left me no time to gather my wits. He grasped me by my hips and pulled me down to the floor, then lowered to his back. I went along with his move, my feet at his waistline before I knelt with one knee at each side of his head. Once on the floor, he grabbed my thighs and centered me above his face.

His bright eyes, now dark and hungry, caught mine. As his mouth moved closer to my pussy, his breath teasing my inner thighs and sending a tingle through my body, he gave me one last naughty smirk and dove in.

I closed my eyes. He slipped his fingers inside me and pulled his tongue from there, moving it all the way up to my clit. I gripped his forearms for support. He circled around my clit, coercing the pulsing nub, before closing his mouth and sucking. Blood rushed from my head to my pussy. His fingers pumped harder, and he did this thing with his mouth that I couldn't understand...

"Oh, God!"

His tongue flicked once, twice, three...five times. I stopped the tally and lost myself to the sensation of each flick consuming me faster and firmer, until my legs were trembling with the building ache. My heart lurched close to my throat and my clit hardened as he kept his mouth in the perfect spot, and pumped...and pumped.

Cold sweats flew down my back. I swayed my hips back and forth over his face, letting his tongue lash at my clit. I gripped his head, trying to center him, but he removed his fingers and plunged his tongue deep inside me.

"James. I'm going to come."

"Mmmm." He sighed around my flesh, thrusting his tongue deeper into my cunt and devouring me like I was his, and only his. He lapped over and over before gripping my clit between his lips.

"You're going to make me come." My breaths were short and uneven.

I could barely see straight as he muffled a laugh before releasing me for a second to say, "Yes, I will," biting me on the thigh to make me wait, then diving back in. I pushed myself against him again, too far gone to hold back the sounds escaping my throat.

My muscles tensed as the sweet tingles started. I let go of his head and squeezed his arms until my fingers went numb. He watched me from below as I rocked above him, pistoning against his face. His hand reached up to my breast where he played havoc until each one ached for more of his rough touch. James pinched and pulled alternately at first one nipple, then the other until I couldn't breathe from the assault.

"Please..."

He closed his mouth around my pussy again, sucking and licking. A spasm flew through my body, then another.

His mouth pulled away for long enough to breathe, "Come, Laura. Now."

After that, his relentless mouth didn't let go until the spasms collected into one giant contraction and triggered my release. The earth-shattering orgasm flew out of my limbs like I'd stuck a fork in an outlet. My toes curled, mouth opened, and I shook until I could no longer stand the bliss and cried out in pleasure and pain.

"Oh, my God! Yes!"

I pulled on his hair, yanking his head away from my pussy while my body spasmed in his hold. My legs shook, my nipples stood tall, and the tightness between my legs continued releasing until the orgasm settled. I opened my eyes and looked down at his glistening mouth. Judging from his smug look of pride, he knew exactly what he'd done to me.

It took a solid minute for my breaths to calm. I slid down his body, sat on his thick thighs and smoothed my hand over the bulging erection underneath his joggers.

In one sweeping pull, he stripped his shirt off his torso. Hard muscles were stacked on top of harder muscles. Every inch of skin was toned, visibly stronger than I'd ever imagined. I held my trembling breath and traced my fingertips down his chest, until I reached his waistband and freed his cock. I wrapped my hand around him. He was hard and warm, pulsing with need, but before my first stroke, he grabbed my wrist with a grunt.

"Not like that, beautiful. I'm not letting you fuck me again before I take you. Stand up."

In one swift move, we were on our feet. He turned me to face the counter where I braced my hands as he left a string of kisses down my spine. I felt him snake back up my body, bending me forward. He gripped my hair into his fist, taking control, and tapped at my inner thighs. I parted my legs, and he whispered, "Good girl."

I loved when he praised me, like he was confirming I was doing the right thing. A low rumble followed from his chest. He lined himself up behind me and slid his cock down my ass crack, then lower into my pussy, sliding all the way in and filling me from wall to wall.

He withdrew and pushed forward, hard and deep.

"Ahh."

I tightened around him and tilted my hips to give him full access as he slid in and out. He finally let go of my hair. His large hand held my hip while the other played with my asscheeks, his fingers getting closer to the puckered hole. The slow momentum sped with each thrust as he pushed deeper and faster, slamming his front into my behind. The sound of slapping skin echoed. The smell of our heat lingered in the air, and I looked back over my shoulder to where his body glistened with sweat.

He pulled me further onto him with each thrust and grunt, wrapping his arms around to my front and holding me tight. We were body to body, our skin glued with sweet sweat.

"Fucking beautiful," he breathed.

I braced my hand against the counter.

"I love having you in my arms and when I watch you take everything I give you; it makes me want to give you more."

He thrust harder, his hips moving back and forth, dick filling me to my depths. But nothing felt better than when he pressed his chest against my back and made us one.

He kissed the spot between my shoulder blades, before trailing his lips down my arm. My grip on James tightened as he moved faster and deeper, knowing exactly what it took for me to reach that beautiful high between pleasure and pain. He confined my wrist behind my back and wrapped his other hand around me, pinching one nipple and then rubbing the other, gently biting my shoulder.

"Are you ready, my nutcracker?"

"Yes." My reply came out like a plea.

He slammed inside me, his cock hitting every sensitive spot and making my body want to melt into a puddle on the floor. I yelped as he played with my nipples, twisting one and moving me sideways to bite the other until they were marble hard. My body was his, tingling from his torment.

"Ah-oh, yes!" The pain mixed with pleasure and passed through me like a wave. He lowered his hand to my front and my pussy, and worked one finger around my clit, winding a tight circle with a featherlight touch, his hips taking a slower rhythm.

I was panting and I didn't want him to stop.

"That's right, beautiful. Just like that. Come for me, sweetheart."

His balls brushed the soaked lips of my pussy, his cock shivered inside me, and I squeezed my eyes shut, concentrating on the feel of him there, and on my clit. His mouth returned to mine, devouring my lips. I froze in the spot, my ass pressing hard into his front.

The hot spasms hit me before I could register them. One after another, they mounted until my knees threatened to buckle under the weight of my orgasm. I yelped out loud and dropped my hands to the counter for support, twitching violently around him. My arms and legs tingled with tiny prickles as I struggled to regain control of my body.

James gripped my ass and held it in his palms, his fingers delving into my flesh. His breath was fast and shallow by my ear as he swore every two seconds between groans, breathing out my name each time he slowed his pace until he was barely moving inside me. He stuttered a final groan and jerked back, spilling all over my ass.

I lay flat on the counter until I felt him wipe me with his shirt. The first feel of cold against my sweat hit my skin and I turned around, covering myself with my bare arms. James grabbed my sweater and pulled it over my head. His breath slowed, but his cock was still rock solid.

"I don't want you to get sick, but that was fucking amazing." His plump lips sought mine as I felt the ground rumbling beneath us. At first, I thought it was my own trembling body.

"You said you're on the pill, right?" he asked.

"Yes."

He sighed in relief and grabbed his pants off the ground.

"But it looks like you caught all your swimmers on your shirt," I joked halfheartedly.

The corners of his mouth twitched upward before subsiding as the earth shook underneath our feet. James jerked into action, yanking on his pants while I threw on my leggings.

My breathing came in shallow gasps as I wrapped my arm around him for support. "Another earthquake?"

The lights flickered. The rumbling roar was deafening and the ground beneath us shook savagely. James quickly shoved me in a corner and used his body to act as a shield between me and whatever was coming.

"It's not an earthquake," he said.

I held onto his arm like my life depended on it. The sound was so loud, I thought the ground would split open at any moment. Then something slammed into the building and a few seconds later, the shaking stopped. The door was knocked off its hinges, and snow blasted into the room. I trembled as James held me against his hot, naked chest until the roar fell into silence.

"Was that an avalanche?" I asked.

"Yeah, that was an avalanche."

The interior door clicked open, releasing the lock.

"We should go. I have to check in on everyone, and…"

I stopped him.

"You can't go naked."

"I'm not wearing my cum." He pointed to the stained shirt before grabbing my hand. We stepped out near the spa entrance, right by the waterfall room. Snow drifted in from above, covering the inside. A scream tore through the hallway from the main lobby.

"Go, go, go," I planted a wet kiss on his lips and let go of his hand. James ran off.

I was about to follow him when I heard a banging on the spa door blocked by the snow. A frightened voice called out for help between sobs.

"I'm here," I said, running around the waterfall to open the emergency exit. The spa was empty, except for a single pregnant woman I'd never seen before.

"You're here on your own?"

"The masseuse went to get extra towels, and then the ground shook, and I was stuck."

She grasped her belly, protecting the baby inside her womb.

"There was an avalanche. We can get out through the back. Is there anyone else here?"

"I don't know. I was lying on the bed, waiting... I... I don't know."

"It's all right. You're fine. Here," I took her under her arm and helped her through the door. "I'll check the rooms. You wait here."

"Okay."

She was shaking like a leaf, but it wouldn't take me long to check for others. I searched every room to ensure the spa was empty before I left. When I returned, the woman wasn't where I'd left her. I rounded the corner, toward the back of the waterfall. The sun filtered through the hole above when I heard James' voice.

"What are you doing here, Tiffany?"

I moved two feet to my right and saw them.

"I told you I was coming." The woman I'd helped stood with her hands on her hips and small belly out front.

"How, Tiff? All the flights were canceled. The roads are blocked."

"When there's a will, there's a way. How could I not come see you when our baby is kicking?"

# Epilogue

### Laura
#### nine months later

Sweat dripped down my forehead as I rushed through the store, searching for something, anything, I'd forgotten to buy for the baby. The world was a blur and my mind raced with an urgency to get everything done at once. With my due date approaching, time was running out before my son arrived.

I registered with a clinic where my parents had no privileges, and since I hadn't seen them in a few months, they still didn't know I was pregnant. As far as they thought, I was busy policing. Truth is, I was afraid to tell them I was pregnant again. But today was the day I would tell the baby daddy that he was going to be a father. Again.

In my hurry through the store, I nearly knocked over a display of onesies, which I caught before they could hit the ground. And that's when I spotted it. A tiny fox onesie, perched atop a shelf, its gray and orange markings bright and cheerful. It was perfect, and I immediately reached out and grabbed it without thinking.

Piercing pain surged through my stomach and I took a moment to rest before throwing it onto the counter. I told the cashier to ring it up. My heart raced and I was breathless, feeling like a mess. I wobbled outside, my arms laden with parcels, and hailed a cab. The driver waited as I dropped off the bags at our shared apartment.

"Where to next, Miss?"

"Manhattan. Silver Brothers Securities."

I took a deep breath and reached for my phone, my fingers quickly dialing Allie's number. She picked up on the second ring.

"Is it time?"

"No, it's not time."

"Oh, okay. You gave me a heart attack."

"You say that every time I call. Listen, I finally decided to tell him."

She screamed something inaudible into the receiver and I waited for her to calm down

"Who is it?" she asked.

"I'm not telling you before I tell him."

"I swear to God, you're not my best friend."

She emphasized the 'not' the same way she had each time I denied telling her about the father of my baby. She had her suspicions, but I never confirmed. It took me eight months to work up the nerve to tell him myself.

"I love you too. Listen, it's probably nothing to worry about, but I've been having some Braxton Hicks and we should probably be ready for this baby."

"Understood. The bag is by the front door, the car seat's installed. I'm ready, Laura. We're ready."

I may not have had a partner for this, but what better partner could I have than my best friend? She was taking her role of a godmother and godfather seriously, sometimes over-the-top.

"I'm on my way to Silver Brothers Securities to see him."

"I knew it!"

"Allie, you promised not to bring it up."

"Got it. This godmother doesn't get to ask questions and—"

"Thank you for not asking questions. We'll go over the birth plan this evening, if that's okay."

"Of course, we will. And once you get home, I'm not letting you out of my sight."

"While we're at it, I would love a foot massage and maybe a manicure. I can't reach my feet anymore."

"Consider it done."

We hung up after confirming dinner plans. Allie was so much more than my best friend. She was my wife, my husband, and my personal organizer at the same time. I owed her for every lie we told to keep this pregnancy a secret. The cab driver pulled up to the curb of the skyscraper, and I felt my stomach drop. This was it; I had to do this. Taking a deep breath, I opened the door and stepped out onto the sidewalk.

The smell of exhaust mixed with freshly cut grass tickled my nose as I made my way toward the building. I had a pep to my step until a family caught my eye and I stopped in my tracks. My heart was racing, and the city sounds around me twisted into one continuous hum. At the corner of the street, there was James, pushing a stroller with Tiffany beside him, and Kensi walking with them, laughter spilling from their mouths.

It was the dream moment I had been longing for, but it wasn't mine. It was also exactly what I had never expected. My research and snooping confirmed they weren't together, but there they were. Together. All too soon, they walked out of view and the spell was broken. Yet, I couldn't move. I couldn't push my feet forward to tell him, or at least go upstairs and leave a note in his office.

A wave of pain washed over me, followed quickly by panic as water leaked down my legs. A moment later, the first contraction paralyzed my limbs and I knew this was it. My baby was coming.

# Chapter 1

## Laura

I searched through the colorful rack of costumes for the perfect Halloween dinosaur outfit. Not for me. For my son. Three years ago, motherhood hadn't been near my radar, but neither was James Silver, the man who knocked me up. Three years later, with a badge on my chest and a best friend for a partner, I was rocking single parenting like Mary Poppins.

"I found it." Allie removed a furry brown onesie with a white-tipped tail. "It's perfect for Foxy."

"No more foxes. He's got a fox toothbrush, PJ, slippers, and bed sheets. It's enough. Foxy needs to get into normal things, like dinosaurs."

"Because dinosaurs are missing from his life."

That tone.

Allie's judgment carried far, but we'd gone through this before. Foxy's father could never be in his life. I dropped my arms to the sides and swiveled on my foot, facing my best friend. The stink-eye she gave me fueled an urge to rescind her godmother title.

"Your mother called—checking to see if you're alive. She hasn't heard from you in six months."

Maybe it wasn't about Foxy's father after all.

"Did you tell her I'm alive?"

"No, I told her she can find you at Evergreen Memorial. Of course I told her you're alive, and I told her Foxy's doing great too."

*She wouldn't.*

My throat seized. "You didn't."

"No, I didn't, but it's about time you told her she's a grandmother. Your father would be happy as well."

"Not happening. I'm not giving my son a grandmother who sends a hundred bucks for his birthday instead of hugging him. No thanks."

"Laura..." She touched my shoulder. "They say a grandmother's love is unlike any other. And since you're a mother now, you have more in common."

"You think that because your mother is great. She gives you love, and you give her...safety and tequila. All I ever gave my parents were gray hairs."

"My mother's a mess just like yours. Maybe a different kind of a mess, but still a mess. Point is, she should know. Maybe she'd surprise you."

I sighed. "I'll think about it, but that's all I can promise. Now, help me find a costume. Our morning break is almost over."

Allie scanned the remaining rack of Halloween costumes. Who was I kidding? I could never rescind her godmother title. She was the best, and she was correct. As screwed up as our family dynamics were, they were still my family, and I missed them. Except, my parents had expectations I couldn't meet. Their disappointment carried all the way from Manhattan and their home in the Hamptons. Avoiding the doctor duo was a challenge, but easier accomplished from further away.

So, I'd kept my pregnancy to myself and now thrived as a single mother. Changing things up wasn't on the calendar, and

Allie confirmed I was alive whenever she answered my mother's calls.

She picked a dinosaur costume, dangling the monstrosity in the air. "A T-Rex with plastic claws. You could poke a kid's eye out."

"Clearly, the fox one wins. It's safe, perfect, and cute." I checked my watch. "And our break is over."

I paid for the costume and threw the bag inside the cruiser. I secured my seatbelt and took a sip of my cooling latte when the dispatch call came through.

"Two armed suspects seen entering the Cameo building near Fifth and Park. All units respond."

I spat out my coffee and fumbled with the cup holder, "Allie, that's us."

My streak of welfare checks and no arrests had earned me the longest time without a bust at the precinct. The snickers behind my back were getting annoying, but today, I would prove them all wrong.

My partner reached for the receiver. "Ten-four. Unit twelve-oh-one in the vicinity responding."

We shot out of the cruiser like two rookies and ran a quarter block to the Cameo building, where we stopped at the corner and assessed the area. A businessman lit a cigarette outside the door. A couple passed a homeless man sleeping on a bench, then entered the building. We watched for clues, but there were none.

"No visible chaos," I said.

"No sign of commotion."

"Seems quiet for an armed entry."

"Maybe they're professionals."

"I'd love to cuff a pro more than I'd like to scratch that two-year-and-nine-month itch."

This was my day. I could feel it in my bones.

"You've had no sex in two years?"

"Two years and nine months. Foxy's conception was my last. This bust is better than an orange in your Christmas stocking."

She looked at me like I was crazy. "Fuck, Laura. That's bad. I bet you forgot how to orgasm."

"Nonsense. I flicked one off under the shower this morning."

"Argh, Laura. I didn't need to know that."

"Shouldn't have asked then. Let's be cautious in there."

I fixed my shoulders back, and we walked to the revolving door. Inside, business carried on as usual. A handful of office workers were waiting for the elevator, and a security guard was sitting at the information desk.

"You think it was a prank call?" I asked her.

"Or whoever ran in here is already upstairs. Let's take the stairs."

"No, wait. Look at the stiff guard."

We approached the desk, and I lowered my voice. "Sir, did you call in an armed entry?"

"Yes—third floor. He's on the third floor. Black hoodie and a patch of silver hair."

My best friend's forehead creased.

"How many exits?"

"He took the south stairwell. North is closed off for renovations."

I scanned the area. Two suits were standing by the elevator, along with a stressed woman who seemed in dire need of a vacation. More entered the front, followed by the homeless man in a black hoodie.

"Clear the area and stand at the front. Don't let anyone else inside until they're all out. Back up will be here soon," I said, and followed Allie's lead up the stairs.

We took the stairs two at a time all the way to the third floor. My chest compressed, my heart hammering and ears drumming with the sound of ticking time. Sweat dripped down my back. The nerves were new; they'd started when I returned to work after my short maternity leave, forcing me to leave my baby with Mrs. Brewers across the street. With motherhood came the additional need to survive for my son. While I was lucky to have a wonderful nanny, she was getting more kids, and Foxy was getting sick more often.

Allie grabbed my arm before I opened the stairwell door. "Laura, please be careful. My godson needs his mom home tonight."

"Fifty percent more police officers died in the line of duty this year than last." The worry coasting over her eyes turned into fearlessness, but I continued anyway. "And since we're not ready to be a statistic, you be careful as well."

She punched me playfully on my arm, and I swallowed past the lump in my throat. "This could be your first bust."

"Not if we keep standing here."

Using her body, she pushed me aside and opened the stairwell door. I followed her down the hallway. After the second turn, a man entered an office. The door shut behind him, and Allie ran forward while I stood in the middle of the hall.

The black hoodie he was wearing was the same one as the homeless man's.

"That's his partner," I said under my breath, but Allie had already burst through the office door. By the time I arrived, she had someone on the ground.

I turned on my heel and ran back to the stairwell. Downstairs, the foyer filled as security ushered everyone outside. I scanned the area, my eyes stopping on the homeless man leaning against a tree. He was watching the exits. I left through the side door and ran around the corner so I could come up behind him. The stretched hoodie over his wide shoulders was the same one as the attacker's upstairs. I removed my gun and aimed at the man's back.

"Hands up!"

His shoulders jerked as he startled.

"NYPD. Step away from the tree and put your hands up."

He lifted his hands in slow motion, palms flat to the front and stance wide.

"Hurry up."

"You've got the wrong man, officer." His deep voice stirred fuzzy memories, but I pushed past the tingling at the back of my mind. I was going to cuff this co-conspirator, no matter what.

"Don't fucking move." I stepped closer. As his arms rose, his hoodie lifted above his belt, exposing a weapon. "Is that gun behind your back registered?"

I removed the gun from behind his belt, noting his tight ass.

"You're under arrest for breaking and entering. Anything you say can and will be used against you in a court of law."

"Breaking and entering? At least make up something believable. I didn't break in."

The cuffs clicked, the final piece of my memory slotting into place.

*Oh, my God. That voice.*

The dread that someone wanted to complicate my life ran through my veins.

"Fox." His name slipped from my tongue.

"Laura? Laura, is that you?"

His head turned with a snap of the neck, and my body went limp. The one man I'd been avoiding for two years was now standing less than a breath away from me. And the best plan my brain could come up with was to take him to the station. If they locked him away for possession, I could kill two birds with one stone: score my bust and disappear. The plan flew through my mind like a stray bullet, until the smell of him invaded my lungs, and the bullet settled near my heart.

"Fox?" His name curled along my tongue. I hadn't spoken

his real name ever, but I certainly held it close to my heart. "I mean, James? Is that you? What the fuck?"

He stood still, as if he shared my shock.

"You're reading my mind. Uncuff me." He twisted sideways.

"I can't. I already read you your rights."

"You mean, you mumbled my rights."

"Shut up. You're under arrest. What are you doing here?" I asked him.

"If I'm under arrest, I believe I get a phone call before I answer your questions, officer."

He was right. And I already knew what he was doing here. My two-way radio confirmed that backup had arrived for Allie. She was getting a ride with a colleague.

"Looks like we're ready to go."

"Laura, take off the cuffs. I'm not the guy you're looking for."

"I beg to differ." He caught onto my hushed breath, and I realized my mistake. The spark in his eyes lit my blood on fire, and I swallowed to clear the rushing heat. It didn't work. I doubted anything would work when his smoldering eyes did their magic. Although the crazy morning we'd spent in Colorado seemed long ago, every minute had stayed fresh in my mind.

"If you run the number on the gun, it's registered to Fox Silver. Take the damn cuffs off, Laura."

His tone drew me out of my daze.

"Ninety-eight percent of criminals try to persuade an officer to remove their cuffs. That's criminal. You're under arrest, and you're coming with me to the station."

"You're making a mistake. I'll be out of the station before you fill out the paperwork."

Backup arrived for Allie, and I directed them inside before I turned back to James.

"Wonderful. Then you won't mind coming along, after all."

"I don't have time for this, Laura. I'm a busy father with obligations who's trying to catch a criminal."

His fatherhood was why I'd left without saying goodbye—and the woman who'd interrupted our stay with her pregnant belly. I wasn't about to compete with the mother of his child, and I wouldn't let my son be second, either. My only other choice was disappearing.

"Laura? Are you even listening to me? There's somewhere I need to be, and if I don't leave right now, I'll miss the appointment."

"All right. We can leave right now. In my cruiser."

"Oh, great. I would really appreciate a ride—"

"I meant *you* in the back of my cruiser."

"You're really gonna do this?" He closed his eyes and took in a calming breath.

A pinch of regret loomed in my chest. "I'm just doing my job."

"Your job?' Anger flamed in his bright eyes. "For fuck's sake, Laura. You were a nutcracker three years ago."

Fury steamed out of my ears.

"Well, then, I guess this nutcracker just got her bust."

I opened the back door and pushed against his heavy body, but he resisted, turning my way. The corner of his mouth lifted, and a dimple sank into his cheek.

*Damn.*

"Will you not embarrass me and let me ride shotgun?"

My heart hammered in my chest, constricting my lungs. A tingling sensation scattered over my skin, reacting to his dangerously sexy tone.

"Rules are rules, Mr. Silver. Suspects ride from the back. I mean, in the back."

Fuck, neither one sounded innocent.

*He smirked.*

"Get in." I gripped his bulging arm and nudged his mass of

muscles inside. Jesus, was he ever strong. I gathered my wits and pulled away from the curb.

"So, what happened to you in Colorado?" he asked.

A better question was, why was the sky blue and his girlfriend pregnant? Why did he seduce me when he had a family, and why did I let him?

*Play dumb.*

"What do you mean, what happened in Colorado?"

I pushed on the gas, throwing him against the back seat. He groaned, and I checked the rearview mirror as he sat closer to the partition between us.

"I mean, why did you leave?" The deep tone rumbled through his chest, and a memory of his beautiful torso flashed through my mind. I cranked the window open for some air.

"There was an avalanche. The mountains got dangerous, and…" I stopped along with the car, waiting for the pedestrians to pass. "And I went to see my sick friend."

I started rolling again.

"And you didn't call?"

I pushed on the brake, and his face pressed against the wired divider. At this pace, we'd never get to the station, but I wasn't about to explain how I despised love triangles and players.

"Look, I had a good time in Colorado, but as you can see, I'm more than a nutcracker now."

"Right—you're a cop who's busting a guy for nothing. Significant improvement."

Was that sarcasm in his voice? I checked the rearview mirror as he rolled his eyes.

"You know nothing about me, Silver. I'm great at my job."

Eighty percent of relationships started with lies; except we had no relationship. I had been good at my job until Mrs. Brewers took another child to babysit. Foxy caught one bug after another, forcing me to cut back on my hours.

"You're definitely great at running," he mumbled and sat back in his seat. I was not about to get into this with him while on the job. Any woman in my shoes would have done the same. I said nothing else until we arrived at the precinct and I put him in a room for booking. I had just signed off on the paperwork when Sargent Dwight called me over to his desk.

"The gun is registered. Mr. Silver's lawyer says you should have checked before booking him for possession."

"He got a lawyer?"

"The Silvers always lawyer up. You would have known that if you followed protocol, which you didn't. I don't want to demote you, Young, but—"

"Demote me? Sir, I know I've been off my game the past couple of months, but I can do my job."

He loosened the tie around his neck.

"You're a good cop, Laura, and I need you here, but you will need to apologize to Mr. Silver."

"So he's walking?"

"Your bust is a no-bust. What do you want me to hold him on?"

Good genes, bright blue eyes, and a body to die for? I shrugged instead.

"I haven't seen you slip like this before. Is something going on at home?"

Did three stacks of laundry, a sink full of dishes, and a sick two-year-old count?

"Foxy's puking again. He's getting all kinds of germs when Mrs. Brewers brings on new kids, so I'm looking for a new sitter, and I'm… I'm sorry about the gun. I won't slip again, sir."

"All right. Go pay your dues and make sure the lawyers are off our back."

"Yes, sir."

I turned and saw him standing by the main desk. He was leaning forward, resting his elbow on the counter, charming the secretary. The overgrown beard was new, but it matched his long lashes. If it weren't for the darker circles underneath his eyes, I'd argue he looked hotter than the night we met. His gaze lifted and caught my stare.

I fixed my shoulders back, lifted my head, mustered my confidence, and straightened my spine, taking calculated steps to the front.

"Hey," I said. "I'm sorry about the power trip. I shouldn't have arrested you."

"Don't worry. I won't press charges if you have dinner with me."

"What?"

"I thought we could catch up."

"Dinner?"

"That's what I said."

"I don't think my boyfriend would appreciate that."

"So you're not single? You're seeing someone?"

"Yes."

Sometimes my lies came out so beautifully. How could I deny the talent? Besides, didn't he have a family to worry about?

The disappointment in his eyes stopped my next breath. I didn't expect the sudden clench around my heart, either. The precinct door opened, and I thanked the lord for some air.

We turned to the entry at the same time. A blonde bombshell was pacing down the hall like it was a catwalk.

It was her. The woman from Colorado.

Her long, flowing dress clung to her delicate curves, and her hair fluttered in the draft. Her earrings matched the diamond tips in her long nails, and her purse matched her shoes. I rarely noticed such details, but it was hard not to notice hers.

"There you are, Fox. I can't believe they impounded your Bentley. We're running late, and I have the car running. I'm going to sue whoever is responsible for this."

That would be me. Normally, I didn't stoop to begging, but I would if it meant I'd keep this job.

She hooked her arm underneath his, but he peeled her clingy fingers off one by one. What was her name again?

"Thanks for coming, Tiffany."

*Right. Tiffany.*

"Ms. Tiffany, I'm sorry for keeping Mr. Silver so long—"

"You're the one who did this?" She eyed my badge. "Officer Young?"

"Yes," I turned to James. I'd rather swallow my pride here than have Tiffany sue me. "I should have never arrested you. I'm sorry."

His chin lifted, and he winked. "My offer stands, Officer Young. We have a lot to talk about. Have dinner with me."

Tiffany took hold of his hand and pulled him toward the door. "Come on, Fox. We don't want to be late."

He stopped, retreated a few steps, and pointed with his finger like he was giving a lecture. "The gun is not the only thing you were wrong about, Laura."

Sergeant Dwight came up from behind me. "I left my wife's homemade cough drops on your desk. I hope your little boy feels better soon, Laura."

My lashes flipped fully open while James's eyes tightened at the corners.

"Ahem, thank you. I've got to go."

I darted to the back room and waited until James Silver, aka Fox Silver, aka my son's secret father, had left with his baby mama.

Continue with Laura and James on their sizzling adventure in *Silver Fox*, Book 6 in the *Silver Brothers Securities Family Saga*.

Silver
FOX
USA TODAY BESTSELLING AUTHOR
LACEY SILKS

**ALSO BY LACEY SILKS**

***Silver Brothers Securities***

Silver Santa

Silver's Rebel

Silver's Pawn

Silver's Secret

Silver's Trouble

Silver Fox

Silver Hunter

***Dirty Deeds Series***

Dirty Cowboy

Dirty Mechanic

Dirty Con

*Be the first to know!*

*Visit www.laceysilks.com*

# ABOUT THE AUTHOR

USA Today Bestselling Author Lacey Silks crafts riveting romantic suspense filled with heat, spice, and pulse-pounding tension. Many of her endearing characters are inspired by her own life, and her loved ones often find themselves playfully woven into her tales. Her two children and her dog, Kygo, keep her days lively with homework queries and affectionate slobbery kisses (courtesy of Kygo, of course).

Outside of penning intense love stories, Lacey is an avid camper and skier. Naturally an early riser, she often finds herself reaching for coffee over water, crediting her billionaire heroes for her packed schedule.

Lacey's characters, replete with flaws and quirks, evoke laughter, sass, and emotion on every page. She cheekily measures men by their foot size, has a penchant for sultry lingerie, and harbors dreams of exploring the nation in a motorhome.

# ACKNOWLEDGMENTS

To my readers, I hope you enjoy Laura and James' story as much as I enjoyed writing it. Christmas is one of my favourite times of the year. I love spending time outside in the snow, and inside by the fireplace with a cup of hot chocolate, catching up with family and friends. I should write more Christmas stories because they are cozy and filled with happy family moments, and just feel good.

To my amazing editor who always finds the time for me, thank you for making my life easy and my writing understandable. Silver Santa wouldn't read the same without your help.

To my beta readers, thank you for your keen eyes! Once I read a story twenty times (or more), the details aren't easy to spot. Your feedback is invaluable and makes the novel what it should be.

To my family, thank you for your constant love, support, faith, and encouragement.

Maya, thank you for your artistic eye and cover design. I'm honoured to watch you grow and develop as an artist. Alex, your loving heart and sense of humour are a constant inspiration. To my parents, this book would not have happened without you. Thank you for believing in my dreams.